Magnetic North

About the Author

Reader. Author. Caregiver. Potato aficionado. Probably an alien.

Marie Bassette has been writing and telling stories since she was old enough to fathom it. When she isn't writing, you can find her taking orders from her cat, getting dangerously competitive at digital word games, and saying "ow!" or "sorry!" because she once again got lost in thought and forgot the dimensions of her physical existence.

Magnetic North

Marie Bassette

BELLA
BOOKS
2022

Bella Books, Inc.
P.O. Box 10543
Tallahassee, FL 32302

This is a work of fiction. Names, characters, businesses, places, events and incidents are either the products of the author's imagination or used in a fictitious manner. Any resemblance to actual persons, living or dead, or actual events is purely coincidental. The publisher does not have any control over and does not assume any responsibility for author or third-party websites or their content.

Printed in the United States of America on acid-free paper.

First Edition - 2022

Editor: Heather Flournoy
Cover Designer: Sheri Halal

ISBN: 978-1-64247-394-0

PUBLISHER'S NOTE

Dedication

Dedicated to everyone who wouldn't let me quit until they knew what was in the box.

"There is no beauty in the finest cloth if it makes hunger or unhappiness."

—Mahatma Gandhi

CHAPTER ONE

"Oh my god," I whispered. "This really happened."

I snuck a peek at North, whose lithe body was tangled in the sheets beside me. I wasn't sure I wanted to believe where I was or what was happening, but between the sun streaming warmly through the massive windows and the obnoxious chiming of my cell phone's alarm clock, I had no choice but to face reality.

"I'm afraid so," North said, half sitting up. The sheet slid down a little, revealing the soft skin just above her breasts. A powerful longing shocked me as my mind was flooded with memories of their taste. We had somehow made our way from the company's dinner to her huge, air-conditioned apartment. From there, my memories were vague.

North smiled wryly and I hurriedly looked away. My cheeks were burning, a mixture of embarrassment and confusion. I was afraid to move, guarding my body militantly from her eyes in the light of morning.

North seemed detached enough about having me in her bed, despite my never having been to her apartment before, but I felt too vulnerable. I blearily took in the sparsely collected furniture of her spacious bedroom. The end table alone was probably more expensive than my car payment and rent combined.

"How did we get here?" I asked, searching my mind for memories of the night before.

It was scary not knowing. I couldn't believe how calm North was being. I felt very sure that life as I knew it was over. Her burnt chestnut curls slid over her shoulders as she turned from me to check the time.

"Could you turn that thing off?" North asked curtly.

It was a tone I recognized. Commanding, but still husky with sleep. North continued talking even though I wasn't prepared for her words to become real in my mind. "Taxi, if memory serves. We were—"

"Wasted. Yeah," I said, glaring at her as I grabbed my phone. "Obviously."

North's lips pursed in a tolerant smile, and she rolled out of the ridiculously luxurious bed. Her long legs carried her briskly across the room, where she began rummaging through the huge closet. I watched her stealthily from behind the screen of my phone, secretly disappointed when she hid her radiant body in a silky wine-colored robe. I was confused by my desire to put her back right where I found her. Why would I even think that when I just wanted to get the hell out of there?

North disappeared briefly in the closet, searching for something she didn't seem to be able to find. When she emerged again, I let my eyes devour her before she turned her cunning gaze on me again. I felt like a visitor to a foreign country and knew I should be a more gracious guest. It was probably a mistake to be lashing out at her, but she was taking it in stride. Almost as if…

"Have you done this before?" I blurted. "I mean…with a woman?"

"No," North said firmly, sitting down on the edge of the bed. From her tone, it seemed as if she had reassured me of this a hundred times already. Apparently, it was getting old.

"I'm in so much trouble…"

I dropped my head into my hands, trying to hold back a flood of hot tears as I considered the life I had just thrown away. It had been a great job. I was comfortable with the people I worked with. Apparently too comfortable.

"Don't worry," North said, my hands suddenly in hers. "I won't fire you."

I looked up, my shimmering eyes peering into her face. I'd never noticed how kind it was before. I had always been so focused on her beauty. And her ferocity.

"It's not just that," I said, pulling away from her gentle grip. I looked down at my phone on the bed between us. A notification was flashing on the screen. Four missed calls. "I have a—"

"Boyfriend. Yes, I remember."

I thought she was teasing me, but her expression softened when I met her eyes. The pain I was feeling must have been visible on my face. I'd have to tell him. We'd break up. Everything was ruined.

North shifted, looking down at the bed. I recognized her brainstorming look immediately and felt a nauseated twinge in my stomach.

"You can call him if you like," she finally said. "Let him know—"

"Let him know what? That I'm naked in my boss's bed? No thank you."

She pursed her full lips again. I had the feeling that if I kept talking, they might disappear completely.

"—that you're all right."

"All right is a bit of an exaggeration."

I didn't like the pitch of my voice, so I was sure North didn't either. I was usually so conscientious about the way I spoke to her. She could destroy my career with a word, but somehow, I was beyond caring. "I'm not all right, North. I might never be all right again!"

"You're being melodramatic, Aria," North said, her cool demeanor as composed as ever. I cringed at the sound of my first name coming from her lips, recalling how she had said it last in a low moan as she climaxed around my hand. I groaned in discomfort as another flash of heat made its way unwelcomely through my body.

"Call me Finch," I grumbled, desperate for some sense of familiarity as my eyes searched the ground for my clothes. I had to get out of there before anything else happened that might threaten my sense of normalcy.

"Fine," North said, as if indulging a small, spoiled child. The tone annoyed me, but when I looked at her, I could tell that I'd hurt her feelings.

"I'm sorry." I sighed, leaning against the headboard of her massive bed. "I just feel so guilty..."

"From what I remember, this was all your idea," North said, that ghost of a smile playing her lips. "Your exact sentiments being, 'Fuck Thom, he doesn't even feed the cat.' And then you passed out before we even finished."

My cheeks burned hotly with the fact of the matter, which finally brought her suggestion of a smile into an outright grin. She was toying with me.

"I did?" I asked, my voice small. I don't know why I bothered asking; it sounded just like me.

She nodded, draping a long leg over my stomach and mounting my body. I inhaled sharply as I felt the heat of her middle against my abdomen. The scrape of her neatly groomed pubic hair against my bare skin, but I restrained myself. North hovered over me, brushing the blond hair away from my face as her mouth dropped to my ear.

"You did." The sheer force of her tone caused my hips to buckle against her, and the flush on my cheeks deepened. A physical testament to my desire dampened her thigh. I wouldn't be able to fight my way out of it with the evidence still hot against her leg, so why was I trying so hard?

"Nguh..." I was all out of snappy comebacks, and she grinned, kissing the nape of my neck gently. I hated myself for not having the power to resist. "But work..." I tried weakly.

"Don't worry," she said, her hand disappearing under the sheet. I closed my eyes, gasping as her fingertips slowly disappeared inside of me. "I'm giving you the day off."

* * *

North and I had fallen into a light, postcoital slumber. Mine was haunted by images of Thom, dressed, for some reason, like my childhood Sunday school teacher. He was shaking his head in disapproval, a deep frown on his face.

"Fuck you, Thom," I said to him. "You don't even remember to feed the cat."

I woke up feeling absurdly annoyed at my boyfriend, despite being the one who had just orgasmed powerfully for another person. Up until that point, things had been okay with Thom and me. We'd been dating a few months. I wasn't considering that he was "the one" yet, but he was all right. He didn't smoke or listen to maudlin country music or anything, and the sex had been okay, so I was holding out hope.

But all that was going to change too. I would have to tell him what happened. Or at least break it off with him. If I was willing to throw him under the bus for a terribly planned night with the woman I'd admired professionally for the past six years, I was clearly incapable of committing to him.

North stirred as if she could sense my wakefulness and opened her dazzling brown eyes. They locked on me, and, as if dissatisfied with what she found, she slid out of the bed. I was shocked once again by her unbelievable body. It seemed to radiate and hum, almost as if it were alive by the very merit of its perfection. The childish feeling I'd had so often that morning came back as I found myself tempted to look away, certain I might get in trouble for enjoying this moment. There was no way someone as immature and inexperienced as I was should be allowed to look at or touch her. And yet…

I expected the same gentle tolerance that she had shown me earlier in the morning, but all traces of the vulnerable woman were gone. She, too, seemed to be seeking the normalcy in our routine, and had readopted her collected, ball-busting attitude. I could tell everything I needed to know about her mood just by the way she walked toward the private bathroom without a glance at me. She hesitated in the doorway before she entered.

“We left our clothes in the living room.” North was unashamed of her nakedness but chose not to look directly at me when she spoke. Instead, she kept her back toward me and her hand on the doorframe. “I’d serve you breakfast, but that’s really something I reserve for people who allow me a first-name basis.”

And with that, she shut the door.

CHAPTER TWO

The walk of shame.

Even though North wasn't there, I wrapped my arm around my torso, hoping to hide as much of my nudity as possible as I ran out the bedroom door. There was a small hallway directly outside of her bedroom, where the narrow walls were decorated with beautiful, framed art. I paused to study a painting that stood out to me, forgetting for a moment that I was in a hurry to get out of there.

I must have looked at it a little bit longer than I meant to, because soon I had the sensation of being watched. I turned, surprised to find North standing by her bed. She was quietly gazing at me as I studied the painting, her face strained by an emotion I couldn't pinpoint. When she realized I'd caught her looking at me, her expression softened for a moment before regaining its businesslike composure.

"See you Monday," she said, as if she had nothing else to say to me.

She really was giving me the day off. I would have laughed if I didn't feel so humiliated.

I hurried to the living room and gasped as the beauty of her apartment struck me once again. I was sure I had been rendered speechless the night before as well, but without North beside me breathing life into her belongings, the luxuries of the room seemed clinical…almost sterile. But I supposed that wasn't too far off from her personality.

I didn't have to look very hard for my clothes. The place was spotless, and the bunched-up lingerie and little black dresses stood out starkly from the plush white carpet. Apparently, things had gotten heated on the couch. If I searched my brain hard, I could probably remember what happened, but I was in a hurry to get out of there and back to real life. I didn't *want* to remember.

I took a deep breath before plunging my hand into the clothes, my heart thudding anxiously as I untangled mine from hers. North's lacy black brassiere brushed my hand, soft like a whisper, and fell to the floor.

I closed my eyes. Sure, I was furious, but was I furious with her or with myself? I had always considered myself a type A personality and had only started to doubt that after finally meeting North in person. In her, I saw the type of woman who really got things done. Who I wanted to be. Would I ever have what it took to cut out personal pleasure for professional success? And if I did, would I be lonely enough to bring women home from the office too?

I pushed the thoughts away and slipped my clothes on, feeling a bit overdressed for my trek home. I would have to take a cab to the restaurant where North had been hosting the company's dinner so that I could pick my car up. The idea of returning to the scene of the crime made me feel sick. It was where we had gotten to talking and stayed talking long after everyone else had finished their meals and were ready to go home.

North had seemed so much more approachable to me then. So warm and lively. Intoxicating. If I had known this would be the result of getting closer to her, would I still have tried?

I couldn't remember at what point the alcohol had taken over, or how she had managed to entangle me in her sensual web. I might have been able to collect my memories if I didn't feel so much pressure to flee the scene. I cursed at the door, realizing that I'd left my cell phone in her bedroom. Would she bring it back to me at the office, so I didn't have to face her again? I couldn't be sure. But if I didn't get it now, I would have to spend my entire weekend cut off from the rest of the world.

My heart was pounding in my ears as I headed to her bedroom one last time, praying to everything that was holy that North would be in the shower and we wouldn't have to interact again. The door was partially open, and again I felt like an invader. I rapped quietly on it and was startled to hear her voice, soft and faraway, reply, "Come in."

I pushed my way in and stood awkwardly in the doorway. North was brushing her teeth, her long brown hair dripping wet and her body covered in a pair of tight black boy shorts and an oversized button-up shirt. She looked sexy, even with a toothbrush in her mouth.

North raised her eyebrow at me expectantly, another look I knew well. She wanted me to hurry up and say what was on my mind. She had things to do.

"Sorry, I forgot to grab my phone."

North nodded, walking back into her bathroom to spit out the toothpaste. She rinsed her mouth out and returned just as I was trying to make a quick escape.

"Finch," she said. Now I cringed at her use of my last name. We'd slept together, after all. But it was my fault for being the one to cut off the intimacy. Was it guilt I was feeling?

"Hmm?" I dropped my phone into my purse and dared to meet her eyes.

"Do…do you need a ride? Or a shower, maybe?"

Her face seemed sad. The whole thing was just too excruciatingly awkward. I shook my head, hoping she wouldn't see the falter in my smile.

"It's all right. I'll get a cab and shower at home. No clothes to change into."

"You could—"

"No, it's okay," I said. "Thank you."

We locked eyes, exchanging an intense look I couldn't pinpoint. She nodded formally and I took it as my cue to go. With any luck, I would never have to look back.

CHAPTER THREE

It was nearly noon before I finally made it back to my apartment. I'd never been so relieved to walk into the cramped little place, but my relief was short-lived.

"Aria!" Thom exclaimed. He rolled off the love seat, plopping to the ground and scrambling to his feet. I had forgotten that he had spent the night and stuck around after I'd left for the company dinner. Apparently, he had been waiting up for me.

I groaned inwardly as he tried to smooth his shaggy auburn hair.

"Morning," I said, probably more sourly than I meant to.

"Where were you?" Thom demanded, dropping an alien-feeling kiss on my forehead. I cringed at the stubble brushing against my skin and pushed him away as gently as I could without revealing my irritation.

"Out," I said. I didn't owe him an explanation.

He seemed dissatisfied with this response and was quiet for a moment.

"Must have been some party," he said, his eyes level on me. I was suddenly positive that he could smell the sex on me. Maybe I should have taken North up on that shower after all. But it was too late. If I was caught, we could end things right then and it would save me the trouble of worrying about it. But I wasn't feeling up for the inevitable fight.

"I'm pretty beat," I said, stepping out of my shoes before heading beyond the foyer of the small apartment. "I'm going to shower and get some rest. We can talk more later."

I thought he was going to challenge me, but instead he surprised me with a lopsided smile.

"Okay. I'm just glad you're home safe."

He went into the kitchen whistling, and I shot daggers at his back. He seemed to feel right at home in my space. And if he were truly oblivious about what I was doing, then I couldn't help but resent him for being so naive. Naivete was a weakness.

Weakness was the number one thing North couldn't tolerate in another person. She seemed to think that if we were willing to remain ignorant and naive, never questioning anybody else's motives, then we got what we had coming to us every time. What must her life have been like to grow up and come to such a heartless conclusion?

Still, in Thom's case, I couldn't help but relate to her. Was it true that you merged energies with the people you slept with? I wondered what I might have adopted from Thom if that were the case. Probably my desire to drink like a fish the night before.

I slipped out of my clothes, dropped my glasses on the rim of the sink, and got into the shower, relieved to be washing away the evidence of my tryst. My mind was whirling, and I just wanted it to stop.

North was my idol. She had been long before I began working for her company. She was about three years older than I was and had established herself in the business world firmly and without compromise. She'd been able to insert herself into the public eye and gain support from women and men worldwide as she fine-tuned her business sense and promoted her unique vision for the future of her company.

I'd studied North in my final year of college during a course on successful women in business. I remembered the first time I saw her picture. I had stared at the gentle slopes of her face and the serious, determined eyes that looked out from a frame of brown hair. She was posing with a challenging smile.

"She's *hot*!" a male classmate shouted out.

The class dissolved into giggles as the professor attempted to regain order. I could see why he would say so, though, and instead of being annoyed at him, or even laughing along, I couldn't stop staring. I was officially drawn in. I set to work learning everything I could about North Acquati. I was shocked when I found that we were so close in age, and that her business was right across the Indiana state border, headquartered in Chicago.

I did my internship with a rival company in the same field called St. Peter's Innovators. They were piggybacking off North's idea to merge social media and environmental technology. St. Peter's were free-trade supporters that were constantly coming out with green products: cleaning solutions, household supplies, furniture, clothing—you name it. The gimmick was that they put people in the Western world in touch with the developing nations that they claimed their proceeds would help. They'd stolen North's idea to make an online presence and created social media profiles for young adults who claimed to benefit from St. Peter's work.

From the outside, it made St. Peter's look, well, saintly. From the inside, though, it had all seemed artificial to me. For a CEO to be demanding a crushing workload on their employees, spending extravagant amounts of money on high-tech building expansions, and the painful marketing expenses...they didn't even recycle.

They had taken North's direct approach to bettering the world and turned it into a self-important mission to sell their sustainable shoe polish. Where she had chosen to utilize word of mouth and grassroots marketing, utilizing social media to really get to the heart of issues that mattered, they had chosen instead to utilize the image of starving people to increase their sales. I hated the ethic behind it, but North had always been very gracious about them in media statements. Besides, her strategy was unique and confidential. She clearly wasn't threatened.

Somehow, North was able to recruit some of the brightest and most creative minds from all around the world to contribute to a line of sustainable products that she was working on introducing to impoverished countries. Her company was famous for their socially conscious approach and innovative solutions.

North Acquati was an inspiration. I'd hoped my experience with St. Peter's would give me the experience I needed to be hired in the main branch of Acquati Technologies. When I finally got settled into my new apartment in Chicago using savings from the barista job that had gotten me through school, I was sure I would land the position. I quickly secured an interview and went in as confidently as possible. But the interviewer took one look at my credentials and sent me packing.

I waited in the lobby for my cab in tears, until North walked in through the revolving doors like a vision from a dream.

"What's the matter with you?" she asked, quirking an eyebrow. The clicking of her expensive high heels came to an abrupt stop. She expected an immediate answer and seemed impatient with the lump in my throat. I was more than a little starstruck but tried to get my bearings fast.

"Your interviewer wasn't impressed with my resume," I said with a sheepish laugh, trying my hardest to wipe my tears away with the back of my hand without dropping my papers.

"Hand it here," North said, snatching the folder from my hand. She flipped through it quickly, then scowled. "Fucking Sandra. Rejects anyone prettier than she is. Come in tomorrow morning at ten. I'll have someone waiting to train you."

North continued into the building as if we hadn't just spoken, glancing at her wristwatch and muttering about Sandra under her breath. And that was how I started working for Acquati Technologies.

I stepped out of the shower and into my bathrobe. I pushed into my cramped bedroom with a surge of frustration and flopped onto the bed without bothering to change into my pajamas. North would probably laugh at my tiny apartment. I heard a soft knock on the door and Thom poked his head in.

"You smell like booze, so I thought you might need this," he said, tiptoeing to my bed and placing a hangover cure on the end table. "It was like my best friend in college. Got me through a lot of long nights and longer mornings. Anyway, I've got to head to work. Stay hydrated!"

He leaned down to kiss me, and without being able to help myself, I kissed him back. He left and I heaved a heavy sigh, wondering why I felt disappointed to have him erase the impression left on my lips by a woman I thought I was desperate to forget.

CHAPTER FOUR

The weekend had passed far too quickly. Thom had tried calling a couple of times, but I let it go to my voice mail. I still didn't know what to tell him. It seemed easier to avoid him, so that's what I did. I eventually got so nervous every time my phone made a noise that I turned it off and resigned myself to spending a very quiet weekend home alone.

I hoped that if I played my cards right, I wouldn't have to go out at all until Monday morning. Unfortunately, by the time Saturday night rolled around, the impossible nature of this goal became very clear to me. My refrigerator was usually restocked around now, and Thom had done me the favor of ensuring that not a crumb was left over during his lonesome sleepover. He'd puttered around the apartment for nearly two days without me there, and he was a muscular man with a huge appetite. I was cleaned out.

The Farmers' Market was every Sunday, so I decided to check my purse to make sure that I had enough cash to stock up. None of the stalls took credit, and I didn't want to go to any of the local supermarkets. I had gotten on a major health kick in college, shedding the majority of the weight I gained from playing with code in my spare time rather than making friends in the real world. The habit had followed me throughout my six years of corporate success. I treated my health foods kind of like a good luck charm.

I rummaged through my purse for my wallet, surprised when my hand struck an unfamiliar object. It was smooth and unnaturally cool, like a polished stone or something metallic, about the size of a brick, and I needed to use a surprising amount of strength to lift it from the bag. Shiny black wrapping paper clung loosely to it by a single piece of Scotch tape as I held it up to examine it. A silver box. The rustling of the wrapping paper drew out a memory that surfaced as if it had been weighed down deep in the waters of my drunken mind.

"I don't normally do this," North said, leading me to a deserted area of the crowded restaurant. I watched her curiously as she pulled a small gift that looked like it had been packaged for the set of a movie and handed it to me. "So, don't say anything about it. To anyone. I mean it. And don't open it until you get home."

She smiled mysteriously and walked away, disappearing into the tinny clamor of the restaurant. I held the package gingerly, stroking its corners and contours, wondering what in the hell North Acquati would be giving me. And why? She wasn't exactly known for her generous spirit in the office. In fact, she was generally a ballbuster.

"Finch, dessert!"

My coworker Lisa interrupted my thoughts. I dropped the gift carefully into the depths of my purse, still burning with curiosity. I wanted nothing more than to dip into the perfumed women's room and tear the wrapping paper off. But I didn't. I wanted to show North, as if she could see me, that I could be calm and collected too. And so, I pretended nothing had changed and held my breath as I merged into the buzzing wall of voices.

* * *

I sighed heavily, plopping onto my couch and studying the box. I had been trying so hard not to think about the night I'd spent with North, but the box was jogging my memory. It was all too embarrassing. I had approached her, already tipsy and emboldened by the strange act of generosity. It made her seem more approachable somehow, as if there were a crack in the wall of ice that she kept between us all.

The more I drank, the cozier I got with her, until we were sitting at a private booth and chatting. I was oblivious to everybody else, and they soon began to scatter, heading home once North paid the bill. I grew bolder the longer we were alone and kept pressing her. All night, North had expertly avoided my questions about the gift, changing the subject with the finesse of a delegation expert.

I was frustrated at first but soon found myself lost in the flow of easy conversation. Her long fingers brushed on my arm as she laughed, staring into my eyes with a predatory intensity, as if she were examining me and learning all she needed to know. I might have been put off by it if I hadn't been dulled by the alcohol, but I was under her spell.

I don't know how long it was before we were in her apartment, but the nauseating smell of leather was wafting in the air and I scowled into her eyes. North raised her eyebrow at me, pausing on her way to the kitchen.

"I can't stand leather," I said, wrinkling my nose. "The animals…"

"Oh," she said, looking at the ceiling thoughtfully. "I'll get rid of it."

I was surprised, but not as surprised as when she was sitting beside me. Somehow, we were on a different couch, or she had draped a blanket over the one we were on. I was far too drunk to remember clearly. All that had made an impression on me was the sparkling champagne on her sleek glass coffee table, and the knees of her long legs nearly touching mine.

Then came the intoxicating laughter, and the feeling of pure satisfaction from cracking her stony face into a smile. I felt like

Moses parting the Red Sea. It seemed sometimes that North was incapable of such a warm, human act. I'd never experienced a sense of power the way I had from making her laugh. I had succeeded at life.

"What did you give me?" I finally asked, drunkenly rooting through my purse and waving the black gift accusingly under her nose. Her hypnotic laughter stopped suddenly and the composure that was starting to drive me crazy lifted North's chin. She tilted her glass regally to her lips.

"Open it, then," she said, as if I were doing it to my own detriment. Her voice seemed laced with frustration, and she kept her eye on me closely. I felt like prey.

"Fine," I slurred, undeterred by the change in her demeanor.

I tore the paper off like a kid at Christmas and stared dumbly at the little metal box. North watched silently, sipping her champagne as I studied the box from all angles. There was a latch with a keyhole in it and I tried to pry it open despite it, disappointed when the box remained steadfastly closed.

"What?" I mumbled. "What's the point of that?"

North's icy face melted into a smile, and I felt relieved that she was still capable of warmth. Unfortunately, I wasn't sure if it was because she still had the upper hand or if it was because of the way I was pouting, as if the super awesome toy I'd been hoping was under the tree had actually turned out to be a jumbo pack of socks.

"You have to earn the key," North said softly, taking the box gingerly from my hands and examining it herself. "There was a note, but…Anyway there's something I need your help with. Something that only you can do. Inside this box are all my secrets. And if you do what I ask of you, they'll all be yours."

I tilted my head dumbly. This was all too much for my drunken brain to process. Maybe if I had been sober, I would have been prepared with a better response, but as it was, all I could focus on was the gorgeous woman who had been my inspiration for so long, somehow trusting me. Needing me.

"You couldn't have just gotten me socks or something?" I asked, pulling the box away and turning it around with a disappointed frown.

Musical laughter flew from North's lips, and she studied me with a look I was almost bold enough to perceive as adoration.

"Not this time."

"Hmm. Well, what do you want me to do?" I asked, gazing at her stupidly.

"I want you to put that thing away," she said with a soft laugh. "We weren't supposed to deal with this yet."

"But—"

"You asked what I wanted you to do. So, I'm telling you. Put it down and kiss me."

And apparently, I'd obliged.

CHAPTER FIVE

Sunday evening came swiftly after a long day of coding Acquati Technologies' latest project. I'd fallen behind a bit because of the day off that North had unexpectedly given me, and I felt like it was important to pick up the slack. I didn't want her thinking I expected special favors because of what had happened between us.

My stomach growled loudly once I finally broke away from my computer. I had been eating like a rabbit over the past three days, and now that I was getting back into my routine, I felt like I was starving. I binged on my very healthy farmers' market food. Anxiety had left me picking at little scraps of food with disinterest, but I was feeling back in control and less shaken by the encounter with North. My body seemed to roar back to life, appetite and all. I sprawled in front of the television set after dinner, my stomach bursting at the seams. Soon, a small pair of paws was pressing on it and the full weight of my cat, Bilbo, abruptly sank onto my already heavy stomach.

"Ohhh, god. Hey, buddy."

"Mrewr."

We sat like that for the rest of the evening, watching old movies on a channel devoted to bringing a blast of the past to new generations. Before I knew it, it was time for bed. In the morning, a new work week would begin. Whether I liked it or not, I would have to turn my phone back on and set the alarm, just in case I pressed the snooze button one too many times and couldn't drag myself out of bed.

As I'd expected, my voice mail was completely full. I listened impatiently as I heard Thom speak over and over again. I cut it off every time, not caring to listen to what he was saying before I deleted the messages. My thumb was pretty trigger-happy by the time North's unmistakable voice rang out from the earpiece. I usually felt insulted when my phone asked if I was sure I wanted to delete a message, but I had never been gladder than when it asked me whether I really meant to hit delete.

"Finch. Come in early Monday. I need to talk to you."

I thought I heard North sigh just before the receiver clicked and cut our worlds off from each other.

I held the phone in a daze, debating whether or not to save the message. Somehow, I couldn't bring myself to delete her voice. I set the phone on my dresser, wondering what in the hell was left to talk about. My heart began to drum, and I suddenly felt very sure that it had everything to do with seeing each other naked. North was a "no loose ends" kind of person. She probably wanted to clear the air and make sure we could still work professionally together. If not, she would end up getting rid of me.

I wasn't sure I was ready for it. Not if it meant risking my job. And would it kill her to *ask* me to come in, and drop the commanding voice for once in her life? Going in early was the last thing I wanted to do. She could at least *pretend* it was optional.

I was startled out of my thoughts by the shrill ringing of my cell phone. I answered it automatically, the absurd notion that it might be North driving me to act before thinking it through.

"Aria," Thom exclaimed. "It's about time! I was getting worried about you."

"Hey," I said as noncommittally as possible, though on the inside I was groaning. "Worried?"

"Yeah…wondered if alcohol poisoning did you in or something. What kind of boyfriend would I be to just, like, let you die in a pool of vomit?"

"Hmm…a bad one?"

"Awful," he agreed. "So, you might have noticed I've been calling a lot—"

"Not really," I said sarcastically. He went on as if he hadn't heard me.

"But there's a reason. First of all, yeah, the dying-in-puke thing was starting to freak me out. Like, I couldn't sleep. And B, I got us tickets for Baba French tomorrow night."

"Baba French?"

"Yeah…they were pretty hard to get, sooo…"

"Are you serious?" I asked, suddenly forgetting North for the first time in three days.

"Death-by-puke serious."

Baba French was my favorite artist. She was an all-around entertainer and performer who rarely went on tour, so when she did it was special. I hadn't even known she was touring again, let alone in my own city the next day.

"Thom, I have to tell you something before I agree to go anywhere with you," I said, squeezing my eyes shut. It was time to take the plunge. The whole honesty thing was harder than it sounded.

"I have a feeling I already know." Thom's voice was suddenly low and serious. "And honestly, I don't want details. We've never had the whole 'dating exclusively' talk. I don't like you because of who you do or don't sleep with, you know. I just like spending time with you because of who you are."

"Thom…" I tried to swallow the lump in my throat. I had no idea what to say.

"Can I just pick you up at eight tonight? We can break up after the concert if it makes you feel better."

I could hear him smiling on the other line and I felt my own defenses melting.

"I...guess so. I'll see you at eight."

"Good," he said, and left me in my bedroom in silence.

CHAPTER SIX

I pulled into the parking lot of Acquati Technologies, my hands trembling as I gripped the steering wheel. I hadn't felt this nervous since I'd first come in to apply for the job, though the training session afterward was also terrifying. It had been hard to believe I'd been handed my dream job by North herself. I was sure I would mess it up immediately and they would all see that I didn't belong there.

It was strange to see the parking lot nearly empty. A jolt of panic shot through me. Was I too early?

No. There was a luxurious black car parked in North's spot. As long as she was there, we could get it over with, and the earlier the better. I didn't want anybody overhearing anything we had to say to each other.

The reception area of the tall building felt bigger when it wasn't filled with bustling bodies. For the first time, I missed the presence of my coworkers, their faces serious as they shuffled on to the next task. It was bizarre to go into an empty elevator, and even more so to be confronted by an unflattering image of myself after spending so much time over the weekend avoiding my reflection.

I'd never much liked the mirror in the elevator, but it seemed particularly invasive today. I had dressed down as much as possible, hoping to look as casual as I could. I tried to avoid looking at the messy ponytail I'd thrown my hair into and the thick glasses perched on my nose. I'd chosen the nerdiest pair I owned in lieu of contacts, hoping they might turn North off and keep the conversation professional. She had commented more than once on the oceanic color of my eyes.

I made it to the top floor, surprised that North's secretary was already hard at work. She didn't seem nearly as surprised to see me, though, and buzzed me in immediately. North was standing across the room with her back to me, staring pensively out the giant window behind her desk at the Chicago skyline.

"Finch," she said without budging. "About time."

"I..."

"Take a seat."

North finally strutted toward me, choosing to lean against the desk rather than sit across from me. She had her long dark hair tied tightly behind her head, looking more assertive than I'd probably ever seen her. Maybe she was having the same weird conflict I was having and wanted to keep things professional between us. I wouldn't have faulted her for being a bit overassertive.

"I'm sure the details of the latest project are fuzzy, considering your state when we last discussed it," North said, directing a teasing smile at me. "But I was hoping to get you onboard without too much ceremony. You seemed fine with the project after a few drinks, but let me ask you again while you're sober."

My stomach was in knots, and I found myself gripping the armrest tightly, trying to keep my gaze from falling anywhere below her eyes. Not only would it make me look and feel submissive, but I didn't trust myself with the tight contours of the black blazer that was hugging her body. Fortunately, North seemed oblivious to my internal struggle and carried on.

"I'm working on something that I don't want to include the rest of the company in on yet. The fewer people who know, the better. So, if what I tell you leaves this room, so help me god, Finch, your career is over. Capisce?"

I nodded, my chest tight. I wasn't getting a great feeling about any of this.

"You might or might not realize that I hired you for several reasons, but most notably I needed you here for your technological experience. Considering the nature of the company, your skillset is something I covet. In fact, you surpass the most experienced person on our Geek Squad."

This was news to me. Since her company was so rooted in social media, I assumed that she had much more experienced people on her IT team. My face must have betrayed my feelings, because she smiled.

"Surprised?" she asked. I shrugged. "Your training here has been specially tailored to your skills. Something that will invariably benefit us both."

"What do you want?" I asked. The discomfort of being in her presence was excruciating. I was on the edge of my seat, ready to bolt at the first given opportunity. North, who had never liked being interrupted during her self-important monologues, sighed.

"I want you to sign a confidentiality agreement," she said.

Confidentiality? I knew this was about keeping my mouth closed. Damn it. A hot flame of anger surged through me and I stood up, staring her in the eye.

"Seriously? Was that all you could come up with?"

"I beg your pardon?"

"You want me to sign some contract to shut me up, is that it? Wouldn't want anyone to know the leader of Acquati Technologies is a rug muncher?"

"Aria—"

"Let me guess. In the fine print, it would say that if I don't keep my mouth shut, my life is over, right?"

"You might just be the most paranoid, self-hating person I've ever met." North leaned against her desk and folded her hands over her chest. There was an air of amusement lurking behind her eyes and I suddenly felt very foolish.

"Um. That, or you meant it about there being a secret project," I said, feeling behind myself for the arm of the chair and sitting down heavily.

"Of course there's a project," North said, staring at me as if she'd just discovered a new, mildly grotesque species. "But I can't give you any other details until you sign the agreement."

"Hmm," I mumbled, my cheeks burning. North pursed her lips.

"We could call your lawyer in if you wish. I'm sure you'll need help understanding the legal jargon for 'my boss is a rug-munching extortionist.'"

I groaned. Her words were venom, and for some reason they penetrated every barrier I held up to protect myself.

"Sometimes I hate you," I whispered, looking down at my hands.

"Then I'm doing my job right."

We sat in silence for a moment as I considered what North was asking. There was a resigned look on her face that was hard to pinpoint, as if she had to try hard not to come out with what she was really thinking. Or maybe my words had wounded her. That seemed doubtful.

"All right," I finally said, my mind returning to the mysterious box she had given to me. If I signed, I would probably learn more about it. My curiosity had finally gotten the better of me. "I'll sign it."

"Great!" North exclaimed, flashing me her winningest smile. I was lost in her dazzling teeth for a moment, unable to shake a heavy feeling of presentiment. Somehow, I knew that in the last few moments, my life had changed forever.

CHAPTER SEVEN

Rainbow-colored lights flashed in the dark amphitheater as Baba French gave her final bow. The crowd was deafening around us, begging her to perform a third encore. Unfortunately, it was clear that she was exhausted and had already given us her all that night. She reminded me of an energetic ferret as she wove around her band on the stage, dancing and performing brief skits and heart-wrenching ballads. The crew was taking the instruments away. She was done for real this time.

The crowd hadn't given up hope, though, and Thom grabbed my hand. We started out, hoping to make our way to the parking lot before the stampede of bodies forced us into a pulsating herd that moved at a snail's pace. We charged to the exit, both of us laughing as we pushed through stubborn fans who were positive Baba would come back to the stage. I secretly wished to be one of the devoted and knew I would kick myself if she began singing again and we'd lost our places. But on the other hand, I was exhausted after my early morning with North. I hadn't learned anything more about her project, and being in the same building as her was energy intensive. I was ready for the familiarity of home. Home wasn't complicated.

"What did you think?" Thom asked as we climbed into his car. He stuck the keys in the ignition and grinned at me as I buckled my seat belt. My body was buzzing in a combination of excitement and fatigue.

"It was amazing," I said, closing my eyes and basking in the experience. I wasn't sure I'd be able to open them again.

"Good," he said, pulling out of the huge parking lot of the venue. "So, are we breaking up?"

I was caught off guard by the question and sat up abruptly. He seemed to think of it as a joke, but it sobered me. Did I really want to end things with him, even when he had been so understanding? I needed someone in my life I could rely on. Someone who wasn't my confusing, female boss.

"I don't think so," I replied. I meant it, but I still couldn't shake the guilt. Did he really still want me, even after I'd slept with someone else? Would he throw it in my face later? It seemed dangerous to believe that he would just grin and bear it. Then again, maybe he was one of those open-minded guys. He'd been able to land Baba French tickets after all. That took hanging around a very specific crowd. What else didn't I know about him?

"Perfect," he said.

My apartment was dark when we arrived, and I tripped over my shoes as I kicked them off and stumbled inside. Thom was right behind me, and I pawed at the wall for the lights. Before I found them, Thom's arms were around me. My breath was taken away as he swept me deeper inside the darkened apartment, a gentle, lingering kiss tugging at my lips. He pulled away, leaving my lips buzzing. I wanted more, so we stayed tangled together in the darkness as we clumsily pushed our way to the bedroom.

I fell back onto the bed with a laugh and he followed, climbing on top of me. I tried to rationalize it for a moment, but it was too frustrating. There was too much to think about, not only about North but about Thom. Was he right for me? Could I trust him? I didn't know and realized quickly that the only thing that felt good in the moment was careless surrender. I didn't have the answers. And maybe sex wouldn't be the answer. But it felt good. That was enough.

And yet, when it came time for my climax, I was ten miles away from my apartment, lying in North's bed as her sinuous body poured over me, keeping me captive to my own forbidden desires. Thom was what I was supposed to want, but the terrifying truth was becoming more and more clear. North Acquati owned me.

CHAPTER EIGHT

"I need to talk to you."

North's voice rang out like a shot behind me, shocking me from my work into a wild alertness I'd only ever experienced during the few panic attacks I'd had during university.

I tried to ignore my leaping heart and appear as casual as possible, turning to face her in my swivel chair. She was studying my cubicle with distaste but cleared her face to a blank slate when she realized I was watching her.

"What's up?" I asked, swallowing hard. I held her eye, even though I was sure both of us were thinking about the same thing.

"Not here," she said as if confirming my suspicion. I wondered why she wouldn't just send her secretary or a memo if she wanted to speak privately in her office. It seemed weird that she would come down into the trenches just for a visit. But we had slept together. Maybe that changed the game.

"Where, then?"

"Follow me."

I stood, reluctant to part from the progress I was making on my work. Still, the allure of time alone with North was too tempting to resist.

She led me to the elevators, and we ascended quietly. There were a few other people in the elevator with us. I expected to go all the way to her office at the top, but we halted a few floors beneath it.

"This way, Finch," North said impatiently, ushering me through the doors. She didn't stop to wait as she began zigzagging through the winding halls of a floor I had never visited before, her black heels clicking purposefully as she moved forward. The halls were mostly lined with private offices, the kind with closed and locked doors and milky windows you couldn't see into.

It was a relief to have North ahead of me. I didn't feel like she was watching me, judging me from behind, and I could study her at my leisure without feeling like she would stare me down. She was wearing a formfitting black skirt today and a teal blouse that made her olive skin look darker than usual. I could feel a flush creeping across my cheeks and groaned angrily at myself, overwhelmed once again by her fierce beauty.

Finally, North settled in front of a closed door and the clicks of her heels stopped. She pushed the door open and smiled broadly at me.

"Welcome to your new office," she said, presenting the room with flair as if it were a prize on a game show.

I stepped inside, my heart hammering in my chest.

"You can't be serious," I whispered.

The room was bright and spacious, nearly as big as her own office. The large window faced the same direction, too, and I realized I'd been given the coveted eastside view. People worked their asses off to get an office like this.

"I'm always serious, Aria," she said.

"Why do I doubt that?" I asked absently, taking in the little details of the room.

Bookshelves, filing cabinets, huge blinds for the huge windows…it was like a subsidiary paradise. I stopped to study the empty oak desk, running my finger along the smooth, cool wood. It was a far cry from my plastic cubicle.

"The desk is only empty because you're a programmer…I figured you'd want to work with your own machine. But if you want a new one—I mean, is that all right?"

It was odd seeing North second-guessing herself and I caught her eye, catching her off guard.

"Is this some kind of preferential treatment?" I asked. "Because I'm not comfortable with—"

Suddenly, North's hands were on my shoulders and she pinned me back against the desk. I dropped onto it with a soft thud, her face inches from mine.

"Why? Because I fucked you?"

I stammered and she held my gaze, back in control with that annoyingly sexy smile creasing her face.

"I wish you'd quit fixating on that," North said.

I was about to reply, but she interrupted me.

"When I'm giving you preferential treatment…" My finger was suddenly engulfed by the sensual heat of North's mouth and I gasped at the unexpected pleasure. "You'll know it."

She unpinned me and stood up, checking her reflection in the window behind me and straightening her blouse as I caught my breath.

"The office is necessary for your promotion. Which, as you apparently forgot, we discussed at the dinner."

A vague memory corroborated what she said.

"This is all mine?" I whispered, getting shakily to my feet. My head was spinning, but I had to keep my feet on the ground. "For how long?"

"For as long as you've earned it," North said. "There are some files in the filing cabinet over there that I need you to enter into the database. There are instructions."

"But my computer—"

"I'm having it sent up now," she said, crossing the vast empty space of the office and standing in the doorway. "That's my next task for you. If you have any questions, you know where to reach me."

North started out toward the hallway before pausing as if she had forgotten something. She turned, a playful smile on her full lips. "Good luck."

She disappeared into the hallway, closing the door behind her. I could hear the clicks of her heels descending as she left me in the huge office alone to process what had just happened.

CHAPTER NINE

The first week in my new office was hectic. The workload was tremendous, possibly more intensive than anything I'd done for Acquati before. There were countless folders of papers to go through, each with individual instructions. I was determined to steam through them, though, and came in early every morning and stayed late every night to make my way to the end.

I hadn't spoken to North directly even once as I went through the motions. I was working by day and spending whatever little free time I had with Thom (who was starting to get a little bit better about feeding the cat). Still, despite my stern warnings to it, my heart leapt every time I heard someone approaching the doorway to my office or I logged into my email account and saw a new message. I only got an email from her once. It was a curt, very North-like message reminding me that the paperwork should be done by the end of the week if we were to progress on schedule.

She still hadn't told me anything new about the project. It made me anxious, but in a way, I was relieved. Without new instructions, I wouldn't have to bend to the pressure of her ever-lofty expectations. I was still off the hook.

It didn't last as long as I would have liked. Before I knew it, Monday morning had rolled around, and I got an email telling me that the paperwork had already processed over the weekend. I sighed. North was an odd sort of businesswoman. She didn't believe in a five-day work week, which I knew back in college and had admired—in theory. Now that I was under her thumb, though, it was easy to feel crushed beneath her overwhelming work ethic. Still, it was part of the reason she was so successful.

I had just settled into my desk that morning and barely had enough time to wonder where to begin when a gentle rap on my door startled me. North poked her head into my office with a pleased smile.

"Aria, great job on meeting your deadline. May I come in?"

She asked as if I could possibly say no.

"Of course," I said.

I was actually glad to see her this time. The data she'd given me didn't make any sense. The shorthand and data values were obscure and confusing. I'd had several questions, but none were so urgent that I couldn't complete my work without answering them, so I'd left them on the back burner, choosing not to seek North out myself. The space was doing me some good.

North closed the door with a gentle click as she entered. She sat down in the chair across from my desk, crossing her long legs gracefully. It was strange having our roles reversed, but I had to admit that I was enjoying it.

"The data you gave me is nonsense," I blurted, unable to hide my exasperation.

She gazed at me as I pushed my glasses from the bridge of my nose to the top of my head. I could feel the nose pieces tangle in my thick blond hair and cringed. I'd have to deal with it after she left. Tucking them on my head was a bad habit I'd found impossible to break, even though they got caught in my hair nearly every time. Now that North had seen me with my glasses on once, I felt more comfortable in them around her.

"I didn't ask you to understand it," North said, cocking her head. "I just needed you to enter it. The files should be shredded immediately now that I know you did it properly."

"North, what am I doing here?" I demanded, my eyes fixing on her over the piles of folders stacked haphazardly on my desk. She sighed and leaned back in her chair.

"I need you," she said, visibly uncomfortable from the admission. I was surprised she wasn't scowling.

"I need to know why," I said firmly. "I signed your stupid paper. Now you can tell me. What the hell is all of this? And what's in that box you gave me?"

"Forget the box for now." From the stubborn tone in her voice, I knew she wouldn't budge on the subject. "But I suppose I'll tell you what I can."

"Thank you," I said, leaning back. I was starting to like the feeling of control. Between North sitting at *my* desk and answering *my* questions for once, it was a welcome change. She raised her eyebrow at me as if she could read my mind.

"Don't get used to the power trip," North cautioned. "Anyway, the data is personal information on potential employees. The shorthand has to do with their countries and locations. Personal ID numbers. Things like that. Their privacy is of the utmost importance, though. If anyone finds out, it will be a shitstorm. Not just for my company, but for the people I'm hoping to hire and their families as well. Understand?"

"But why?"

"You're going to have to trust me to keep that confidential for now, all right? I chose you for the project because you're competent and discreet. Your talent will help me push into goals I only imagined possible."

"What kind of employees are they?" I asked, ignoring the compliment. North was masterful with her words. If she wanted to hide something, she could dance you right around the subject and have you thanking her for it. If I didn't ask now, I might never get my chance.

"Acquati Technologies is officially branching out," she said, glancing uncomfortably around the room. Was she afraid of someone overhearing? She had secured this room for me herself, so her paranoia was intriguing.

"Branching out?"

It was a surprising relief to have something akin to a normal conversation with her, even if it was one that made her uncomfortable. The awkward, emotionally charged interactions we'd been having were excruciatingly stressful. It had been good to spend the week focusing on my work and Thom. I was starting to feel like myself again, and able to pretend that maybe everything that had been going on with North had been a figment of my imagination. I could handle it. Thom was who I wanted, and North was the terrible mistake. I was in control. I had the power over my life to maintain normalcy.

"I'm setting up a work program overseas. I just need your help with the details. As I'm sure you know, in order to achieve a goal, you have to break it down into manageable pieces."

"Of course," I said. It was one of her mottos, but I wasn't sure where she was going with it.

"Right now, the two of us are building a foundation to make my plan come to fruition. But while the plan is in its infancy, I need to keep it in my head and delegate simple tasks that can currently be accomplished. Once we're almost there, the greater goal should be clear to you."

"Why can't you just tell me your plan outright?" I demanded.

"I did," North said wryly. "You forgot it. And I've had enough time to realize that it's for the best."

"Why?" I was on the verge of whining but tried to keep myself under control.

"I guess I found out my father was right when he said you never really know how fickle a woman is until she's been in your bed."

I stared at North, anger and something else—shame, maybe?—bubbling in my chest.

"You can trust me," I said glumly, biting my tongue this time.

"Like I said, I need you. But don't mistake that need as trust. I can't just trust you with everything. Not yet."

North stood from her chair and gazed at me, her caramel-colored eyes flashing. She wanted to say more but seemed reluctant. Instead, she strutted toward the door and turned to me once she reached it.

"Instead, I'm going to have to ask you to trust me. This is for your own good."

She disappeared, leaving me with more questions than I'd had to start with.

CHAPTER TEN

When I got home, I was surprised to find Thom still hanging out in the apartment. I had been expecting him to be at work. Instead, he was sitting at the bulky desktop I used for work. Even with all the latest technology, I preferred the clunky machine I'd used throughout university. I had learned everything I knew about computers with it. I was really possessive about it, and seeing Thom in my chair made me prickle.

"What are you doing?" I asked, frowning as Bilbo wound his way between my legs.

"Playing a game," he said, turning around and switching the monitor off quickly. He ejected the CD from the tower on the floor and stood, showing me the disc. It was some hack-and-slash game I'd seen in commercials. I scoffed, and he laughed lightly.

"I'm sorry, TV got boring and I just bought this. Also, I made you dinner."

I sighed. "Thanks."

"No problem. But hey, after we eat, I have to get going. Work stuff."

"Okay," I said, trying to hide the relief from my voice. I was really looking forward to having some time to myself for a while. I was still prickling from having Thom messing with my desktop. It would be nice to be alone. I needed some stress relief. Bilbo headbutted my leg and trilled gently. I headed to the kitchen, and he followed at full speed, yowling.

"Did you feed him since you were here?" I asked. I already knew the answer and groaned at Bilbo's empty dish lying on its side on the light blue kitchen tiles.

"Sorry, I was getting to it," Thom said, poking his head into the kitchen as I filled the bowl. "I made lasagna."

He had placed a white candle on the middle of my tiny kitchen table. I usually preferred to eat in the living room since the kitchen was so cramped, but it was a sweet gesture. We ate quietly and when it was time for him to go, I was relieved. He kissed me goodbye, and I saw him out and headed to the shower to wash the memories of the day away and start with a blank slate.

I felt I'd earned my night's sleep by the time I finally fell into bed. Bilbo joined me soon after, and the gentle rumble of his purring lulled me into a deep sleep.

* * *

At around 1:00 a.m., I was awakened by the shrill sound of the vintage rotary phone I'd hooked up to the landline in my apartment. Few people had the number, and I tried to list them as I sat up, lifting Bilbo gently from my chest. He blinked lazily before deciding to follow me as I climbed out of bed and stumbled down the hallway.

"Hello?"

It was unsettling to answer the phone without any caller ID to give me a heads-up of who might be on the line. There was a pause, then what sounded like a sharp intake of breath.

"Aria?"

It was North. My surprise and grogginess were enough to stifle any of the inhibitions I would have had on a normal day.

"North? What the hell? You know it's one in the morning, right?"

I leaned against the wall with my eyes closed. I felt like I could sink back into sleep at any moment.

"I know," North said, taking a shuddering breath. "It's just… we were robbed."

She bit back a sob and suddenly, I was fully awake.

"What? Where are you? Are you all right?"

"I'm at the office. I don't know…I just woke up."

"Jesus Christ…"

"Aria—Finch. I'm scared."

North fell quiet and all I could hear was her shuddering breath. My heart constricted in pain.

"I'm on my way."

CHAPTER ELEVEN

Everything was a blur until I reached the parking lot of Acquati Technologies. Luckily, I didn't live very far away. It was one of the things I had taken into consideration when I was looking for apartments in Chicago. I stepped shakily onto the pavement. The huge building looked dark and ominous, but I was eager to get to North.

Eerie silence blanketed me when I entered the lobby. The only light was coming from the silver glow of the moon and the streetlights outside the building. North didn't keep her building lit up the way most of the other companies did. She practiced what she preached as an environmentalist, and openly bashed other corporations for wasting energy.

I paused, suddenly wondering if North had left the elevator's power on or if I should take the stairs. Memories of the dark, narrow passageway made my skin crawl. It was steep and would take me close to half an hour to make it to the top floor of her skyscraper. I'd have to try the elevator and hope for the best.

Fortunately, the elevator was still powered, though the lights were dim. I paced impatiently as it ascended. By the time I reached North's floor, I was nearly exploding with anticipation. I pushed through the metal doors as fast as I could and burst into her office.

I found North huddled on the floor in front of her desk. The filing cabinet was overturned, and she was timidly sorting out the papers that had spilled from its drawers. Her hands were shaking, and she showed no indication that she had heard me enter.

"North?"

I walked cautiously forward. She looked up at me in the dark, fear etched deeply on her face. I saw with an aching heart that her high, beautiful cheekbone was bruised. It was startling to see her so vulnerable, all traces of her composure gone.

"Finch." She sighed. "Thank god."

North tried to push herself off the floor but I rushed to her side and sat down beside her so she wouldn't struggle to get up.

"Let's have a look at you," I said softly, smoothing the dark hair from her face. Her physical appearance was in just as much disarray as her office, and I had the brief, absurd notion that she truly was connected to her work.

"I don't need a hospital," North said firmly, the strength in her voice challenging me before I could even suggest it.

"Of course not," I said. "You're Wonder Woman."

She seemed thrown off guard by my reply and her features softened.

"I don't know how they got in here," she said. "There were three women. I think. Their faces were covered."

She ran her hand through her hair and a trickle of blood spiraled down her thumb.

"Take your blazer off," I demanded.

"What? Of all the times for you to take the initiative, this is hardly—"

"You're bleeding!"

She sighed, silenced by my look, and peeled the black blazer from her body. The blood was staining the white button-up shirt beneath it from her elbow down.

"How did you not notice that?" I exclaimed.

For some reason, I was angry. Not only angry that she was hurt, but angry that she wasn't able to take care of herself. Maybe angry that I was seeing her vulnerable for the first time and feeling so utterly helpless.

"Well excuse me for having other things to worry about," North snapped back, gesturing to her demolished office. "You know what, Aria? I'm not like other girls, all right? One little boo-boo isn't going to keep me from doing my job."

"I can see that," I said coolly, frowning down at the neat piles of papers she had stacked around her. "Where's your first aid kit?"

North sighed irritably. "I didn't ask you here to play doctor. I just need help cleaning up my office."

I raised an eyebrow and North scowled.

"It's in the lobby. By Sandra's desk."

"Thank you," I said, standing. "That wasn't so hard, was it?"

North pouted at the files and I couldn't help but laugh softly. It was surprisingly comfortable to have the roles reversed, not that I was happy to see North hurt. On the contrary, I was furious that anyone would dare to lay a finger on her. It just felt nice to be able to take care of her for once.

I moved cautiously through the darkened lobby and, after being scared a few times by my own shadow, was able to return victoriously with the first aid kit.

"Where's your light switch?"

"Leave the lights off," North said. "The office is supposed to be sleeping. You know how the media gets. No one should know we're here or find out what happened. That means no doctors. No police. No lights."

I sighed and relented, returning to North's side and rooting through the first aid supplies. I knew that what she said was true. Everyone seemed eager to see her fail. A successful woman somehow posed a threat to a world that many men wanted an exclusive claim to.

I didn't want to be responsible for having her name appear in the newspapers as a source of controversy for a pack of wolves to tear into. It would be the beginning of the end. So, for the time being, I decided to let her have her way.

She didn't flinch or whimper when I cleaned the wound on her elbow. I wondered how hard she had to try to keep herself together as I poured peroxide over the cut. It was a deep gash that left me nauseated. North, ever watchful, pursed her lips.

"You're not going to pass out on me, are you?" she asked. "Because if you are, I can do this myself."

"Shhh."

I started unrolling the gauze around her firm arm, wondering how in the hell she found the time to work out. Before I could finish, I hissed in frustration. The fabric of the blouse was getting in the way of dressing her wound.

"We have to take that off." I sighed. "Looks like we're playing doctor whether you like it or not."

North raised her eyebrow at me and slowly worked the buttons of her blouse. I'd expected more of a fight, but she seemed to be perfectly at ease with the new development. I, on the other hand, lowered my eyes, glad that the office was dark enough that she couldn't see the dark flush creeping across my cheeks.

"Shit," I whispered when she shrugged the shirt off. Her ribs were bruised, and another small cut had sliced right under her breast. Rage and sadness surged through me. "What did they do to you?"

"Nothing I couldn't handle," North said firmly.

"You can tell me."

She shook her head, and I could tell she wasn't going to budge. When North's lips were sealed, they stayed that way. It was part of the reason she had been so quick to get her startup up and running. Her plans and secrets were hers alone.

"Are you sure you don't need a real doctor?"

"I would know if anything was broken," North grumbled. "Now stop fussing over me. I can take care of myself."

I shook my head in exasperation and finished bandaging her elbow. As soon as I was done, North pushed herself to her feet and walked unsteadily to a tall cabinet against the windows. She opened it and I was surprised to see that it was full of clothes. I watched in wonder as North pulled out a crisp white blouse and quickly draped it over her shoulders, buttoning it in lightning speed. She caught a reflection of herself in a mirror that hung inside the door and pulled a hairbrush seemingly out of nowhere.

"What's all that?"

North glanced back at me, startled as if she had forgotten that I was there.

"I spend the night here sometimes," she said reluctantly. "Saves time."

I thought back to her extravagant, sterile apartment and imagined what it must be like to come home from the office to so much space. And yet she was all alone. It was a sad realization.

"No wonder you get so much done," was all I said.

I stood awkwardly while North primped until finally she closed the cabinet and faced me. She had pulled her hair up and out of her face and covered the bruise on her face with a layer of concealer.

"Ready to earn your pay?" she asked.

I nodded, and we set to work in cleaning up her office in the dark.

CHAPTER TWELVE

By the time we finished cleaning North's office, nothing was out of place. I had been trying to convince her to call the police, or at least tell me more about what had happened, but she was steadfast.

"I'm not talking about this. Not right now. Drop it, Finch."

I got annoyed being shut down every time I broached the subject, and eventually took her advice. We worked in silence until, at last, she was satisfied.

We rode down to the parking lot in the elevator together. North looked really fragile leaning against the mirrored wall, and I laced my fingers through hers. She squeezed my hand, and we stayed like that until the doors clamored open and revealed the lobby. We untangled our fingers and pushed through the huge doors and out into the parking lot. North set the security code.

"A lot of good that did," she grumbled. Still, she was meticulous about locking up.

I followed North to her car, catching her when she stumbled. She had been off-balance all night, and it had worried me enough to force her to take anti-inflammatories from the medicine cabinet in case she'd hurt her head. Getting her to admit she was hurt was a new kind of battle, and it left me feeling exhausted.

"Thanks, Finch," North said, pulling away from my protective grasp. "Good night."

"North—"

She paused but didn't meet my eyes. She seemed embarrassed and ready to put the night behind her.

"I think I should drive you home."

"I'm not going home," North said with a sharp laugh. "Whoever did this didn't find what they were looking for, so that will be the next place they go."

"Well, what are you going to do then?"

"I'll just stay at a hotel for a few days until things blow over."

I studied her pale face and frowned as she swayed. North looked completely exhausted. I wondered how long it had been since she'd actually slept.

"I don't think it's a good idea for you to be by yourself."

"I'm a big girl, Finch. See you tomorrow? Wait, it's Friday… Monday, then."

North began walking slowly to her car and I intercepted her. I couldn't believe what was coming out of my mouth. "Come home with me."

She opened her mouth to protest but before she had the chance, I'd already put my hand on her arm and was guiding North toward my car. "Just for tonight. You can do whatever you want tomorrow. I just want to make sure you're okay. Please?"

North tiredly buckled under the pressure and let me lead her to the passenger's seat. She ducked inside and soon we were both shut into my car. It instantly filled with the gentle sandalwood and lavender blend that was North's signature smell. I closed my eyes and inhaled deeply, hoping to still my heart before turning the key in the ignition.

"Let's get you out of here," I said, trying to prepare myself to open up my home to the world-famous North Acquati.

CHAPTER THIRTEEN

As soon as Bilbo heard my keys from the other side of the door, I heard a muffled yowl. I laughed softly to myself as I pushed the door open. Greeting him was my favorite part of the day.

"Never pictured you as a cat person," North said. I could feel her standing close behind me and found myself feeling a little short of breath.

"He's my best friend," I said. "I'm surprised you never noticed the picture I had of him in my cubicle."

"I'll admit, the pictures on your sad little wall were the last thing I was looking at," North said.

A little forbidden thrill coursed through me when her hand brushed against my leg, seemingly by accident as she bent over to remove her high heels and place them neatly beside my rows of worn-out sneakers. The stark contrast made me laugh out loud. Was I insane? A woman like North should be in a five-star hotel room. Luxury suite. Not in my cramped little apartment. Why had I insisted on this? It already felt like a mistake.

North's pantyhose-clad feet padded across the carpet and into my living room, where Bilbo immediately greeted her by winding his fluffy gray body through her legs.

"Traitor," I teased. He trilled at me but continued purring against North's legs. A ghost of a smile appeared on her lips, and I felt a sudden painful relief to see that even after the night she'd had, she could still feel happy. I guess I took it as a sign that she was going to be okay.

"What's its name?" North asked, reaching down shyly to stroke Bilbo's head. He headbutted her hand with force and she laughed. I was dazed for a moment by the beauty of her smile.

"Bilbo."

"Like the hobbit?" she asked, shooting a glance at me. "You're such a nerd."

"That's why you hired me," I said with a tired grin. She returned her attention back to Bilbo and I took the opportunity to slink from the room and into the kitchen, where I poured us each a glass of wine. I figured she could use something to calm her nerves. I knew I needed it.

I returned and handed her the glass. She took it gratefully.

"You're in your pajamas," North stated.

It was funny that she hadn't noticed before that. Where had her mind been? I wasn't sure I wanted to know.

Personally, I was preoccupied with bracing myself for her to comment on my cramped living room and insult my way of life. Every wall was lined with shelves that were full to bursting with books, CDs, and scatterbrained sketches and journals. Nothing about my apartment seemed to be North Acquati's style. She looked so out of place in her extravagant outfit, standing awkwardly in the middle of my chaos like a lost puppy.

"Let's sit down," I said, plopping heavily onto the couch.

North nodded and lowered herself gracefully beside me, sipping from her glass.

"Thank you," she said after a few quiet moments. "If I'm going to be perfectly forthright with you, I wasn't looking forward to spending the rest of the night alone."

I frowned. "Who would?"

"I didn't feel safe speaking to you about this in the office. I'm not certain, but someone may have bugged it. There has been a lot of interest in my comings and goings. Outside interest."

I set my glass on the coffee table.

"Do you know who attacked you? Or why?"

"Not specifically who," she said. "But I do know why. The gift I gave you. They're looking for it. Now that I know how far they're willing to go, I'm afraid I'm going to have to ask for it back."

"What, so they can come back and succeed next time?" I exclaimed. "Not on your life."

"Aria, it's for your own good."

North's caramel-colored eyes bore into mine and she sat her glass down on the coffee table with a soft clink. "Please."

"No way," I said stubbornly. "I've been daydreaming about what could be in there since you gave it to me. I'm going to keep it and I'm going to open it."

"I would never forgive myself if something happened to you because of this," North said, gripping my face in her cool hands. "I can't be the reason you get hurt."

My mouth went completely dry. Every inch of my body wanted to pull her close to me. To hold her tightly and console her for whatever violations she had experienced that night. Maybe I could show her I was strong enough to withstand whatever might come my way. I could keep the box. Her secrets. Everything about her.

But more than that, my need was selfish. I wanted to feel that same intimacy we had shared the night of the company dinner. I was longing so desperately for the heat of her lips against mine. The powerful jolts of rapture she could elicit with just a flick of her tongue. I secretly basked in the memory every chance I got.

I pulled away from her hands and rubbed my temples. What was wrong with me? The woman had gone through hell that night and all I could think about was sex. I was a terrible person.

"What is it?" North asked. "What did I say?"

"It's not you."

"You've been acting so weird around me lately." North sighed. She sounded genuinely distressed about it. "I thought…"

"What did you think? That things would go back to normal?"

"Actually, I was hoping they wouldn't."

The lilt of her voice instantly brought heat to my loins and I crossed my legs, hoping to hide it from her. It wasn't appropriate. She had been through so much. This wasn't the time to go exploring these complicated feelings. Besides, I shouldn't be having any feelings at all. There was an image I had in my mind already. The perfect life.

"I'm not a lesbian, you know. I have—"

"The guy who neglects the cat. Got it."

I finally gathered the courage to meet North's eyes and turned to face her on the couch.

"I've just been really confused," I said. I didn't want to treat her so coldly. Maybe it was time I tried giving her an explanation. Maybe it was the only way I'd ever be able to understand it for myself.

"What are you confused about?" North asked, perking up. She was immediately in problem-solving mode. Apparently, it cheered her up.

"It's kind of complicated. I just feel like this is wrong."

"What kind of wrong?" North asked. "It's important to be specific. Eternal hellfire wrong? Or wrong because it's something that won't serve your life?"

"Wrong…maybe hellfire?" I guessed.

"I grew up Catholic," North whispered, picking her glass up again and taking a deep drink.

"Protestant," I whispered back. North winced.

"Ouch."

"I'm not even religious," I said with a sigh. "But that's not really the issue. I just feel scared."

"Why?"

I looked across the couch at North, whose brown eyes were looking so sincerely into mine that I could have cried. I was afraid of how much I wanted her. Terrified that if things didn't work out, I couldn't let her go. I was worried that being with her would mean saying goodbye to the life I had planned out for myself. That if things went wrong, I could lose the career I had always dreamed about. What *wasn't* scary about being with her?

"Are you afraid of feeling good?" North asked, cozying up beside me. Before I could stop her, her face was buried in the nape of my neck. I sighed involuntarily as her soft lips tugged at my sensitive skin. It left me gasping for breath, and I reached down to take her hand in mine. I had been wanting to hold her so badly that night. Why was it that she was still the one leading things with me? Was it really what I wanted?

"I don't know." I gasped as her fingers worked their way under my T-shirt. "Maybe with you?"

"Why? Because I'm a woman?" North asked.

"You've never let that stop you before."

"And I won't tonight, either."

Her words electrified me, and I exhaled softly as she did the one thing that could have helped her recover from that night. She put herself back in control.

CHAPTER FOURTEEN

We slipped quietly into my bedroom. The room was dark and familiar, a welcome change after the chilling emptiness of Acquati Technologies.

"It's so comfortable in here," North said, fingering the quartz sphere on my nightstand. "It feels like you."

I sighed inwardly, relieved that the cleanest room in my apartment was the one that North felt reflected me the most.

"Do you remember when we met?" North asked, her silky voice far away.

"You mean when you found me bawling in the lobby?"

North laughed, a soft breath through smiling lips.

"I'd forgotten that part," she said fondly, sitting tentatively at the edge of my bed. "You looked so pitiful."

I sat down beside her, my heart fluttering, and laughed sheepishly.

"I meant our first time really talking. When I took you out."

"You mean that official boss-employee dinner thing you do?"

"Yes," North said curtly. "That."

How could I forget? North Acquati's smooth voice, cajoling yet demanding, informing me first thing in the morning that I was going to get dressed in my nicest clothes and wait outside my apartment building for her driver at 5:00 p.m. sharp. I had probably never been so surprised to receive a phone call in my life.

I'd spent the rest of the day fretting over what to wear and convincing myself that I would do something embarrassing I would never be able to live down. When it finally neared five, I chose one of my newest dresses—a long, deep blue gown that I secretly hoped looked attractive on me. I spent the limo ride to the restaurant trying to fight a nausea unlike anything I'd ever felt before and wasn't sure if I was relieved or terrified when we finally arrived. Her driver had led me inside and swiftly departed, leaving me alone in the foyer.

It took no time at all before somebody in a suit that probably cost more than my college tuition led me quickly up a winding spiral staircase. I found myself in a secluded room with a huge skylight and vast windows that overlooked the city. North had always been one for a good view, I already knew. In interviews, she claimed they put her at peace.

As soon as I saw her lounging alone at the table, her long legs crossed beneath a tight red dress, my heart began pounding wildly. She looked like she had just walked off-set of a glamorous photo shoot for one of the business magazines that featured her.

"Is this some kind of test?" I asked as soon as I sat down.

I could have kicked myself for blurting it, but I had already been running through all the scenarios in my head. She was taking me out to test me. To prove I wasn't good enough to work for her. To find some way to make fun of me and confirm my deepest fear—I was poor, plebeian, and worthless, and I had known it all along.

I've never been able to handle my nerves very well. I tend to come off as aggressive when I feel afraid of anything, and as a whole, North terrified me.

Fortunately, she was undeterred, and a peal of musical laughter erupted from her.

"A test?" North asked, unable—or unwilling—to hide her delight.

I was mesmerized by her every movement, and North shook her head, almost imperceptibly. I could practically hear the gears turning in her head, but she didn't let me in on what they meant. North uncorked a bottle of champagne that was in a bucket of ice on the table and poured us each a glass. Her caramel-colored eyes danced long after she took her first sip.

"Thanks," I said glumly, acutely aware that I had made an ass out of myself. Still, I was beginning to feel at ease. I was surprised by how quickly North was able to laugh off the blunder and save me any embarrassment. She was a lot more easygoing than she let on.

I sipped nervously as North sized me up from behind the crystal glass in her hand. Everything she did was so graceful. I felt like I was bombing my chance to make a good first impression, but somehow, with North smiling at me like that, it didn't matter so much anymore.

"Is there anything I should know about you before you come to work for me?" North leaned back in her chair, her eyes steady on me.

"Like what?" I asked, the nervous bile rising in my throat again. I kicked myself for the eagerness with which I'd agreed to join her. Of course she was trying to find out what a nothing I was. Bigwigs didn't just let great careers fall into the laps of normal people like me.

"Allergies? Preferred name? Dietary preferences? Pronoun?" North said, leaning forward expectantly. I was dumbfounded for a moment before I realized it was my turn to speak.

"Pronoun?" I stammered.

North shrugged. "You never know."

"Would you even remember? I'm sure you've asked the same things a million times to hundreds of other people."

"It's all up here," North assured me, tapping her temple with a long finger.

I briefly considered how impressive that was before I was swept back into our exchange. North was a seamless conversationalist, and I had never felt quite so comfortable opening up to anybody before. She was quick-witted and seemed engaged by everything I had to say to her. Even the most trivial of things.

About halfway through the dinner, I went back into panic mode. There was no way I could possibly be having such a good time with my almost-boss. This was the same woman I had looked up to for years. A woman larger than life. How could she actually be enjoying my company as much as I enjoyed hers? Enough was enough.

I held my hand up and immediately brought the conversation to a halt. North's lips tugged into a wry, expectant smile. She was used to calling the shots, and I'm sure she was curious about what I might have to say.

"Is this all for show?" I demanded. "An act?"

"What do you mean?" North asked.

Her flawless face creased in confusion, and I suddenly felt awful. What was I thinking, putting her on the spot for my insecurity's sake? We were genuinely enjoying ourselves. But some self-destructive power in me urged me forward.

"Is this something you do with everyone? Take them to dinner to harness some kind of team spirit? If you pretend to like us, we'll work harder, right? I took a business class too, you know."

North exhaled, her eyebrow arched, and lifted her glass.

"To honesty," she toasted, taking a deep drink. After a moment of quiet (whether she was savoring the flavor or articulating a response, I couldn't tell), she spoke again.

"I do treat all of my employees to dinner before they start. I find it clears the air. We hammer out the details so I can make company events inclusive. They also get to quell their butterflies and ask me whatever questions you can imagine. I learn everyone's individual way of communicating. It's useful for the team as a whole, but personally I like to have a connection with the people who are helping me work on the most important thing in my life."

It was the first of many North Acquati monologues I would ever hear in person. I was terrified that I had insulted her, but she surprised me by beaming.

"I'm not pretending to have a good time, Aria," North said, as if magically able to infer what my question was really about. It was like a soothing balm on my soul to hear her say it. North took my hand in hers and my heart nearly stopped. Her touch brought untold pleasure surging through me. A forbidden heat was rising up, and I had to do anything possible to put a stop to it.

"You should call me Finch," I said, pulling my hand away. If North left my first name out of it, maybe I'd be able to distance myself from the terrifying feelings she gave me.

"All right," North said. She sounded defeated but her smile didn't falter. "Finch, then."

CHAPTER FIFTEEN

The past was left behind when, sitting side by side at the foot of my bed, I tentatively touched North's hand. I wasn't sure what to do with her. I had never been one to act on my impulses the way the men in my life always had. I guess I'd gotten spoiled, having them dote on me and never hiding when they were ready to take me. But with North it was more intimidating. There were no roles for us to play. We were both women, and right then, she was really vulnerable. If I kissed her, it would be taking advantage.

"What are you thinking, Finch?" North asked softly, stroking my thumb with hers. She was smiling at me, and I found it impossible not to return the gesture.

"I was just wondering how women do this," I said, laughing down at my knees. It was excruciating not knowing what to do next, even though I knew exactly where I wanted to end up.

"Hmm," North said, scooting closer to me. Our legs were touching now, and she draped her arm over my shoulder. "I think they might start something like this."

"I think so," I agreed, swallowing the lump in my throat.

"Aria?"

I was startled by North's voice. The vulnerability of the question. I looked into her eyes and frowned.

"What is it?" I asked.

"Do I come on too strong?"

North's eyebrows shot up as I dissolved into giggles.

"What?" she demanded.

I tried to explain but hadn't quite been able to articulate it even to myself. I opened my mouth to try to collect myself but fell short, which led me into more peals of laughter. I felt terrible leaving North hanging like that, but it was too late. I was already succumbing to my most obnoxious childhood habit: giggle fits.

"What?" North cried, more demanding this time. "Tell me!"

But the more she tried to throw her weight around the funnier the whole thing seemed to me. North Acquati was concerned that she came on too strong. The irony of her asking that when, for the first time, she was the one who was being vulnerable, combined with the legitimate absurdity of my attraction for her, was all too much.

I fell back onto the bed and stared at the ceiling, wiping my eyes as the laughter slowly died down. By then, North was actually laughing too, and she scooted farther up on the bed, so she was sitting cross-legged beside me. I cleared my throat and soon North was in my sights, peering down at my face.

"Why are you laughing?"

"I don't know." I sighed, gripping her jaw in my hands. North let out an exclamation of surprise as I pulled her face down against mine.

"What—"

We kissed then, a kiss unlike anything I had ever experienced before. A kiss I never wanted to end. Maybe because, for the first time, I felt like I was in control.

"Well," North said, pursing her lips when we finally parted.

I nodded.

"Well," I repeated.

North sank into the bed beside me, her fingers toying with mine. I turned to face her and was startled to see how tired she looked. It had been a really long night. I brushed the dark hair from her forehead and surprised us both by scooping her up in my arms. North resisted for a moment before finally resting her head against my shoulder and letting her eyes flutter closed.

Soon, her breathing was shallow and pure, and I knew that she was asleep. I was far from it, though. My mind was reeling with the implications. What was North doing in my bed? And what was this unfamiliar tenderness that made me feel like somebody was juicing my heart?

North whimpered suddenly and I held her tightly to me, kissing her forehead. She was soothed for the time being and I swallowed hard, terrified that if I moved, I would somehow prompt her to have a bad dream. I stayed frozen, stiff like a board, blissful but tortured. I wasn't going to move, even if the world was on fire. I could hear Bilbo scratching at my bedroom door, but both of us knew I wouldn't let him in tonight. Even in her sleep, North demanded all my attention.

CHAPTER SIXTEEN

This time, I woke up before North. She was curled up to my left with her back to me, breathing softly and clinging to a scrap of sheet that was pinned beneath one of her long legs. I felt a pang of guilt and cringed, realizing that I was a terrible host. I hadn't even offered her pajamas. Still, North seemed perfectly content curled up in her white button-up shirt and crisp black skirt. I let my eyes linger on the slope of her hips for a moment before climbing out of bed.

It felt like an awkward morning after, despite the fact that nothing had really happened. North had been through hell and I'd comforted her. Anybody would do that. We didn't have sex again. Everything was normal. I could forget about it and pretend I hadn't wanted anything to happen in the first place.

I let myself out of the bedroom as quietly as possible. As soon as Bilbo saw that I was up, he wound himself through my legs and mewed pitifully and persistently—our morning ritual. He followed on my heels as I scrambled to feed him, not even getting a chance to brush my teeth. If Bilbo woke North up, I would lose the few moments of clarity I would have to myself to gather my thoughts and come up with a plan.

I hoped I would have time to shower and dress before North woke up and slipped into the bathroom. My routine felt a little off knowing that North was in the apartment, but I trucked on anyway, trying to convince myself that it was a normal day. Everything was fine. I just happened to have a ridiculously gorgeous woman sleeping in my bed. No big deal.

I stayed under the water a little bit longer than I meant to, but it felt comforting. I was certain of my fate in the shower; on the other side of the door, I wasn't so sure. I knew I had to face her sooner or later and eventually climbed out from under the soothing water, cursing as I realized that I'd forgotten my towel in the laundry basket in my bedroom. Of all the times to be too lazy to put my clean laundry away, of course it had to be the night North Acquati summoned me out of bed to help her clean up after some sketchy midnight robbery.

I couldn't bring myself to pull on the same dirty clothes I'd worn the night before, but the thought of sneaking into the bedroom made my stomach churn. North might have been completely at ease with her body, but the same definitely did not go for me. I didn't want to do anything to lead her on if she was awake, like making her think I felt comfortable enough with that type of thoughtless, intimate display. We weren't nesting. We were coworkers.

Normally, it wouldn't be a crisis. I would have been able to go into my bedroom unabashedly and get dressed. But there was a woman in there I wasn't sure I was ready to face. Especially naked.

I clearly had no choice, though, and consoled myself with the hope that North might still be asleep. I crept to my room and hesitated outside the door, stealing a glance at Bilbo. His round eyes were fixed on me, and I knew in that moment that if he had been capable, he would be laughing. Poetic justice for shunning him the night before.

I pushed my way into the room without thinking, my mind focused on escaping Bilbo's judgmental stare. Somehow in that brief instant, I let myself forget that North was in the room, and we were both startled when I closed the door behind me and caught her eye as I leaned against it, naked and dripping wet.

"Oh!"

North's voice brought heat to my cheeks. She lowered her eyes modestly, but I could tell that she was trying not to smirk. She and Bilbo would probably get along well.

"I forgot my towel," I mumbled, hurrying to my dresser and fumbling through the drawers. "If you need a shower, remind me to get one for you."

"Oh, that's all right," North said, shooting me a sly smile. "I air-dry."

I stammered, trying to articulate a reply, but before I managed, North swung her long legs out of the bed and left the room. I heard the shower running a few moments later and sank down onto my bed with a heavy sigh. She was already making herself at home.

Before long North was sauntering into my bedroom, her radiant body completely nude. I tried not to let myself look at it, but my eyes were drawn to the deep purple bruises on her ribs. Even battered, she was beautiful, but the sight of her wounds made me sick to my stomach.

She was no fool and snapped her fingers at me, directing my attention away from her abdomen.

"I hate to ask, but would you happen to have something I can wear until I get back to my apartment?"

When I looked into her face, I cringed. The makeup she had used to conceal the bruises on her face from the night before had been washed off, and I was left with the unnerving image of a fallen warrior. Fierce as she was, a sneak attack had managed to leave her frail enough to take refuge in my shitty little apartment.

"Of course," I said, standing a little too quickly. I rummaged through my clothes, wondering what in the hell I owned that might suit North. I'd never seen her in anything less than designer.

"Something comfortable if you don't mind," she said, as if reading my mind. I grinned to myself and chose a pair of yoga pants and a T-shirt and brought them to her.

"Do you want…" My face burned as I tried to figure out how to ask if she wanted to borrow underwear. She smirked and shook her head. A flash of heat surged through me, and I tried not to think about having nothing between North's body and me but my thin yoga pants.

I handed the clothes over, my face burning, and looked down at the floor as she pulled them on. Hopefully she wouldn't catch me watching her stealthily with my peripheral vision. I couldn't help myself. I was smaller than North, flatter and athletically built while she was nothing but curves. My shirt was tight on her, hugging her breasts snugly. Without a bra, the impression of her nipples just barely concealed beneath the fabric made my mouth dry. What was wrong with me? I fought valiantly against the temptation she roused in me and struggled to redirect my mind.

"Are you hungry?" I asked.

"Starved," North answered, beaming up at me.

I stared at her, caught off guard by how stunning she looked without makeup. It seemed like no matter what she did or how she looked, I couldn't get enough of her.

"All right," I said, tearing my eyes away from her. I led her to the kitchen, silently praying that I would have something in my apartment worth feeding to the world-famous North Acquati.

It was embarrassing to show North into my small kitchen, and I found myself agitated once again by the cramped way I allowed myself to live. Even my stovetop was full of books and scatterbrained thoughts scrawled on scrap paper. But North didn't seem to mind. She wasted no time making herself comfortable at my tiny table, shamelessly reading some of my Post-its as I rummaged through the refrigerator.

"You know, you're quite brilliant," North said, shuffling through the papers littering the table's surface.

"Could you cut that out?" I said over my shoulder with a sigh. She smirked at me and shook her head.

"This is why I hired you, you know."

"How does lasagna sound?" I said edgily, anxious to change the subject. For some reason, I felt embarrassed and irritated when North complimented me. Part of me felt unworthy, while another part felt like she was mocking me.

"Perfect!"

Her enthusiasm caught me by surprise, so I took out the leftovers that Thom had made for me and put them in the oven to heat them up. I cursed when I realized I had gotten sauce all over my hands and washed them quickly. Meanwhile, North remained absorbed by the glimpses she stole of my secret inner world. Just as I sat down across from her to wait for the lasagna to finish, my phone rang.

I saw my mother's number and answered compulsively. I was always worried that something might be wrong when she called. She did so rarely.

"Aria, honey?" she asked, her voice shrill and metallic from the speakerphone. I struggled to turn it off, but my hands were wet, and the touchscreen wouldn't work.

"Who else, Mom?" I said, smiling wryly at the table.

"Don't be wise, it's not very attractive."

"I'm not trying to be attractive," I replied.

"Of course not, dear. Hell would freeze over."

I glanced at North, who raised an eyebrow at me. My mother had always been after me about my appearance. She thought I didn't do enough with myself and constantly implied that this particular form of laziness was why I was still single. She didn't understand why I would keep my look simple and comfortable when I could get contacts, cake on the makeup, and show up the daughters her friends were always bragging about. Sometimes it felt like she just gave birth to me to compete with other people.

"What do you want, Ma?" I asked, rising from my chair. I could never sit still on the phone with my mother. I always ended up pacing.

"I just wanted to see how my girl's doing. Chicago is far, you know."

"I know." Far was kind of the point. "I'm fine."

"Good. Aria, you know, I heard the strangest thing today…"

My mother's voice took on a conspiratorial tone and I sighed.

"What was that, Ma?" I asked, humoring her despite the foreboding in my chest.

"Nancy's boy, Christopher, was found kissing Jason, Theresa's nephew," she exclaimed, her tone dripping with venomous disgust. "I heard the women in church talking about it. We've organized a prayer meeting for them next week. Nancy's making sure Christopher goes, but nobody can be sure if Jason will stick around. I sure hope he comes…"

I bit back a groan of frustration and turned my back to North so that she couldn't see my face.

"Isn't that something," I stated, my voice strained. I never knew what to say to my mother when she got on her tangents. I almost never agreed with her, but it was easier not to say anything at all than to challenge her beliefs. She was convinced half the world was going to burn in eternal hellfire—including me, if I didn't start wearing more makeup and snag myself a husband before menopause.

"I know! It's just awful. We all feel *so* bad for Nancy."

And yet I seemed to sense a hint of glee in my mother's voice. This was juicy. It made her tiny world feel full.

The timer on the oven went off and I exhaled in relief. Saved by the bell.

"Mom, I've gotta go. I'm cooking."

"You're *what*?" My mother snorted. "Hell must really have frozen over."

"I'll grab a sweater. Talk to you later."

"All right, dear, take care."

I dropped my phone unceremoniously on the counter and sighed deeply.

"I know of a good conversion therapy camp if your mom wants the number," North said. I whipped around, ready to freeze her with an icy glare, but her deadpan face broke out into an understanding smile. "I'm kidding, Finch."

I shook my head and pulled the lasagna out of the oven. When I came back to the table and handed North her plate, she glanced at it for a moment before reaching across the table and gripping my hand.

"Are you all right?"

I sank down into my seat without pulling my hand away from North's. It was warm and comforting. A disarming contrast from my mother's voice.

"She always makes me want to smoke or drink or something," I mumbled. "Heavily."

"Well, that explains a lot," North said, pursing her lips and gingerly pulling her hand away.

I was left feeling lost and alone as North gripped her fork eagerly and started to dig in.

"What do you mean?" I asked, tucking my hands together in my lap.

"Nothing, Finch."

We were quiet as we began eating. I glanced up at North, surprised to see her face contorted in an expression of discomfort.

"What's wrong?" I asked, setting my fork down.

"Aria. This lasagna is atrocious."

I knew I should probably be insulted, or at least horrified that I had served her something she hated, but for some reason her honesty made me laugh. It had been a little bland for my taste too.

"Did you make this?" she asked, poking distastefully at a noodle with her fork.

"Actually, I didn't. Thom did."

"I wouldn't trust a man who makes food taste like this," North said, grimacing as she took another bite. "His heart is black."

"What?" I laughed. "That's a little dramatic, don't you think?"

"No! Italians know," North assured me. "I'm going to feed you *real* lasagna and you're going to see the difference."

North grinned at me, shoveling the rest of her food into her mouth at record speed. She almost gagged as she choked it down and chased it with a long drink of water.

"It's *canned sauce*, Finch. Not even any salt and pepper! He clearly doesn't love you."

"He has no reason to love me."

North's caramel eyes fixed upon me. They were filled with a tenderness that nearly made me cry, though for the life of me I couldn't fathom why. I waited for her to let me in on whatever it was that made her look at me that way, but she didn't speak. Instead, she tore her gaze from mine and laughed sheepishly.

"Look at the time," North said, standing. "I should get back to my apartment. Care to drive me?"

She knew I would before she asked, but we both took comfort in the formality. I grabbed my keys and phone, and together we headed out the door.

CHAPTER SEVENTEEN

"Finch, get the door."

I glared in the direction of North's bedroom, where she had disappeared ten minutes before to rummage through her things. In the time that she was gone, she had called one of her security men and the doorbell rang. Despite my annoyance at North's tendency to order me around, I crossed the room hurriedly, ready to do as she wished.

"Where's Ms. Acquati?" a broad, sunburnt man with a square face immediately asked me. I gestured toward her bedroom, and he pushed past me. I closed the door behind him, sulking.

"Nice to meet you too," I grumbled.

He didn't seem to hear me. By the time I made it back to the couch, I could hear North conversing curtly with the man. I grinned despite myself. It sounded like he was having his ass handed to him. *That's my girl.*

I paused, irritated by the fact that I'd let a thought like that slip past my filters. North wasn't *anybody's* girl. I had nothing to do with the incredible woman she had become, and calling her mine was flawed for more reasons than I could even begin to consider. Besides, I had a Thom. Whatever that meant.

I hadn't heard from him since he had left the last time, and honestly, I had nearly forgotten he was dating me. That was probably a good indication that it wasn't meant to be. Or that maybe I was a little more enamored with North than I was letting on, even to myself.

Fortunately, I had plenty of time to mull things over. North was taking stock of everything in her apartment to make sure that nothing had been messed with in the time that she was gone. Her personal security guards had been posted and before long tens of people were scrambling around the apartment. I started to think that she had forgotten about me, but soon she emerged from her bedroom, her familiar, all-business gait rousing me from my seat.

"Thanks for all of your help, Aria. We can take it from here."

"Are you sure? I mean…"

"No, you've done more than enough. Thank you for being there for me. I won't forget it."

I tried to hold her gaze, but North turned her back on me and headed back to the bedroom. Probably to fight more with the security guard she'd ordered me to let in her house.

I felt a little huffy, dismissed that way, but North was the kind of woman who got things done. I was merely a means to an end. She was safe now. That was all that mattered.

I felt a surge of resentment toward her as I headed home and dialed Thom's number.

"Hello?" his voice said from the passenger's seat of my car. It was almost as if he was sitting beside me, and I inhaled, hoping to forget everything that had happened with North.

"Hi," I said. "I was wondering if you might want to get lunch or something."

"Oh, I wish I could. I'm busy, though. You know the grind."

"Yeah," I said, my thoughts involuntarily turning toward my job. It was hard to imagine working anywhere else, and my job had suddenly become a lot more demanding. It was strange to work under North. Especially now. I didn't even know what I was doing, exactly.

"Well, we can have dinner instead if you want," Thom said. "I should be done here around six. Is that too late? I could cook for you again."

I had to hold back a cruel burst of laughter when I remembered North's reaction to Thom's cooking.

"No, that's all right. I was thinking of going out this time."

"Sounds great," Thom said. "I'll call once I'm off work and we can make plans then."

"Sure. Bye."

"Bye."

Was I imagining the lilt? He sounded like he was hanging up with a girlfriend he loved more than anything. It made me a little bit uncomfortable. Maybe I would tell him about what was going on with North. Just put it all out on the table. It would be nice to have someone to bounce my feelings off, even if it was just Thom. But that might be selfish. I would just have to play it by ear and decide when the time came.

* * *

I spent the rest of my day running errands and doing housework that I wished had been done before North stayed the night. I wondered briefly if she would be coming back, but it seemed like a once-in-a-lifetime event. She belonged in elite towers and VIP rooms. Not passed out in her work clothes on my bed.

By the time six rolled around, I was feeling pretty exhausted. Thom called before I could come up with an excuse to stay home.

"Hey," he said, his tone light and flirtatious.

"Hi," I replied.

"So, where were you thinking to eat? Want me to pick you up?"

"No," I said. If he picked me up, that would lead to him coming back to my apartment. I wasn't sure I was ready to have him there. My bed still smelled like North. "I was thinking I'd meet you. I'm on the road anyway."

I don't know why it felt easier to lie. In truth, I was lounging on the couch with Bilbo, who was kneading at my lap from the couch cushion across from me. Maybe it seemed like if I didn't lie, Thom wouldn't give up on the chivalrous thing to do. But I really didn't want him there, even though it felt like I should.

"Cool. How about that place on the corner that you like? That way you don't have to drive very far to get home."

"Sounds perfect."

"Okay, I'll be there in about half an hour. See you soon."

He hung up before I had the chance to say goodbye, and I sighed heavily.

"I guess that's that," I said to Bilbo. He blinked lazily at me. "Want me to bring you a doggy bag?"

Bilbo's round eyes glared as if he knew how terrible my joke was, and I forced myself off the couch. It was just dinner. And maybe I would get my guilt off my chest and work through these weird feelings. It was worth a try.

CHAPTER EIGHTEEN

I met Thom at the restaurant, and as soon as he smiled at me, I felt an insurmountable guilt. He had acted okay about knowing that I slept with somebody else, but did that make it right to carry on with whatever it was that I was doing with North? I barely understood it myself. How could I expect him to?

"Hope you're hungry," Thom said, kissing my hand and sitting down at the table. Actually, seeing him had made me feel anxious and nauseated, but I couldn't tell him that. I just smiled and sat down.

"I feel like we haven't seen each other in centuries," I said with a sheepish laugh. Even if we had just seen each other a day ago, my mind had traveled light-years since then. It was distracting, whatever this thing with North was, and I was anxious to figure it out.

"It has been a while," Thom agreed. "Working adults and all. But you know what they say. All work and no play..."

Thom reached across the table and stroked my hand. I jerked it away involuntarily and immediately felt bad as his face fell.

"I'm sorry, Thom." I sighed. "I think we should talk."

"Sure," Thom said, leaning back in his chair. "What's on your mind?"

"Well—"

"Are you guys ready to order?"

A waitress, one of the girls who looked more disillusioned by life every time I saw her, was standing at our table tapping her pencil impatiently. She would probably be friendly if she wasn't being forced to do something she didn't want to do. I'd been in her shoes more than once, but I couldn't imagine living like that anymore. Not now that I had my career.

It had always been my dream to do what I was doing. Working with code was like speaking a language that could create entire worlds that had never existed before. I'd had my share of shit jobs over the years and couldn't let my feelings for North jeopardize my future. There was no telling what her whims would have me do next, but Thom was safe. He was happy if I was happy, and that was that. Why was I sabotaging everything I had, not only with him but with my career, for these confusing feelings that I didn't even want?

"Sure," Thom said, smiling up at the waitress. But when he turned his eyes back on me, they were serious.

After we ordered and the waitress had moved on to a table behind us, Thom raised his eyebrow at me.

"So, what did you want to talk about?"

"Nothing," I said, laughing sheepishly. "I just have a lot on my mind right now. Maybe later we could talk about it."

"Well, we could always go somewhere more private," Thom said, his dark eyes studying me intently. I had the absurd feeling that he was trying to read my thoughts.

"Yeah, we'll see," I said, trying my best to laugh brightly.

What was I thinking, wanting to talk to Thom about North? It wasn't like my feelings for her could be anything serious. We

"No, I wasn't doing anything," I said quickly, crossing the room to sit beside her. I wondered if Thom was still waiting for me to come back to the table. "I'm just glad you're okay."

"Aria..."

North's caramel eyes bore into me, and I felt myself suddenly growing nervous. Maybe I shouldn't have been there. But she sounded so scared on the phone. I couldn't risk leaving her alone knowing full well that someone was after her.

Still, I couldn't help but feel frustrated. Weren't there people out there who were better suited to protecting North than I was? She refused to involve the police, but wouldn't she be safer if she did? It was better to be safe than sorry. Why did she have to be so damn stubborn?

"Aria, come here," North said, patting the seat beside her on the couch. I moved forward uneasily.

"In the days to come, you might start hearing unfavorable things about Acquati Technologies...about me," she said, lowering her caramel eyes to the floor. "I don't want you buying into the slander."

Was it possible that rumors actually bothered a woman like North? Or maybe she actually cared about what I thought of her. Both seemed implausible.

"Whoever is behind all of this wants to tear the company down for some reason. I'm sure they're after my research and hope to benefit from it for themselves. I don't know who those women were last night, but I've been thinking all day. I want you to get rid of the box I gave you. Throw it into the river. Anything. Just make sure it's gone. I'm serious about this."

"Not until you tell me what it is and why," I said. If North could be stubborn, then so could I.

"We've been through this. A lot of it is data," North said impatiently. "Important information about my company. Secrets I can't afford to get rid of yet. Not until the programs have been completed."

"How long do you think that will take?" I asked, frowning. If this didn't get off the ground soon, it was impossible to tell what kind of danger was facing North. Especially if she refused to get help.

"I really have no idea, Aria. That depends on you. I need your help setting up the programs. I thought it would be a good idea to trust you with the rest of the information. But whoever is behind this has surely seen you with me by now. You have to get rid of it."

"I can't just toss it, North. Not if it's that important. Anybody could find it and hold it against you. Or just steal everything you've worked so hard for. I'm not going to let it happen. I'm the only one helping you set your program up."

North looked suddenly guilty.

"That's not entirely true," she said, pursing her lips and glancing away from me.

"What do you mean?"

"I mean you're not the only one helping me."

I felt sick suddenly, as if she had somehow slapped me in the face.

"There's also my brother. Donnie."

I don't know why I felt so betrayed in that moment. North had help. Why would she ever trust everything with me? She thought I was fickle. And there was a good chance that I was. But I couldn't help the fact that it stung.

"Oh," was all I could say.

"I was thinking about introducing you two, but so far the time hasn't been right. He's visiting my parents in Italy."

"Your parents live in Italy?" I asked, suddenly recognizing that this was a chance to get to know North better. It was an opportunity rarely afforded to anybody.

"Yeah," North said. She grew dark suddenly and I felt sure I had crossed a line asking her about her personal life. I was about to apologize when she continued speaking.

"My sister was killed last year. My twin. Afterward, my mother developed some health problems, so my father is taking care of her in the village where they grew up."

A twin sister? I wasn't sure I could handle a world with two women like North in it.

"You never talk much about your family," I said, keeping my thoughts private. "Especially in front of the media."

This was a rare opportunity indeed.

"It's nobody's business, and my family wish to remain anonymous. I want to respect their privacy. Of course, the media hounds have a way of finding things out, so I think Italy was a practical choice for them as well. As soon as somebody caught wind of my sister's death, they would have hounded us all mercilessly at a very vulnerable time."

"I'm so sorry," I said, gripping her hand. Her fingers stayed loose, and when I looked into her face, she was gritting her teeth. Was that the way she kept herself from crying?

"Anyway, just get rid of the box, would you, Finch? I don't need anybody else I care about getting murdered, all right?"

I was caught off guard and pulled away from her.

"That's out of the question. Would you rather lose another sibling over this? Because he's the only one who would be able to hold on to the box for you."

"Jesus, you're stubborn! I'm asking you from a good place, Aria. It's not like I'm happy about this."

North glared at me, but I didn't let her intimidate me. I kept pushing.

"I know, but if the project is that important to you, I'm going to keep my promise."

"That doesn't matter anymore. There's no way you're not in danger. I wasn't just scared for myself tonight, Finch. I was scared for you too. I'd just feel better if we…I want to keep you in sight for right now, okay?"

I looked into her sincere brown eyes, shining with unshed tears, and nodded. "Okay."

North sniffled, an almost imperceptible sound, and squared her shoulders.

"Finally, you're sounding sensible."

I pursed my lips, readying myself to reply, but she had already gotten her way and wasn't going to acknowledge the conversation anymore.

North stood triumphantly and shot me a devilish smile. "Right. Let's have a drink."

CHAPTER NINETEEN

I should have known enough by then not to drink with North. The warmth of the alcohol loosened my tongue and made me feel game for anything. Without inhibitions, it was easy for me to put things in black-and-white terms. If I wanted to do something, I did it. If I didn't, I would fight tooth and nail not to. There was no overanalyzing involved. It eased the burden of my quick, anxious mind.

A similar change seemed to come over North. Her tension disappeared, and I could imagine I was speaking with her the way I would have if we had met as children on the playground. She was fun and uninhibited, and the icy glint in her eyes melted into warm honey.

I found myself wishing that she would always be like this with me, ready to laugh or take my hands into hers and drag me around, just as she was doing that night. I was getting the VIP tour of her apartment; North marching purposely forward with me in tow and showing off her favorite trinkets in her collections.

I was amazed by her artistic eye, and the display cases in her home rivaled those of every museum I had ever been to. We were peering down at a handful of colorful gemstones and laughing about Neanderthals when suddenly I blurted what had been on my mind for the past couple of weeks.

"You're so beautiful, North."

North laughed, clearly delighted. "You can't hold your liquor, can you, Finch?"

I surprised us both by gripping her shoulder and thrusting her against the display case. Her eyes flashed, filling me with heat as I pinned her down, my face inches from hers.

"Lucky for you," I said, prying her legs apart and reaching greedily between them.

North gasped and immediately I was gratified by her heat. She moaned as I gently massaged her, losing herself in the pleasure of my touch. What had taken me so long to touch her? I should have pounced on her the second I walked through the door.

"Not here, Finch." North gasped, pushing me away and straightening herself. "The neighbors will see."

"Neighbors?"

I turned clumsily and stared out the huge windows. Yes, North was one for a good view. And we would be giving whoever could see inside quite the show. You could never tell who might be peering in with binoculars, especially when the condo across from yours belonged to a gorgeous, successful woman like North. It made me feel scared for her. Protective.

"You didn't seem to care the first time," I mused, heading back to the huge living room.

"That was before…"

North trailed off and suddenly I remembered why I was there in the first place. Somebody was after North, making her life a living hell. And here I was, a bumbling drunk, taking advantage of her once again. When was I going to get the story straight, even in my own head? Why did it always feel like one or the other of us was being predatory? Sex was complicated.

No, sex with *women* was complicated. With men, it was always clear in my experience who was the predator and who was the prey. But with a woman like North, the comfort of those roles was lost. It gave way to a completely new feeling entirely. It stopped feeling like a game and started feeling more like a need. Or an addiction, maybe. I couldn't get her out of my head for five seconds. I only seemed to be happy when we were touching. Otherwise, my brain went all topsy-turvy. But it was an addiction I had to abandon my comfort zone to indulge in.

"You okay, Finch?" North asked. From the tone, I knew her eyebrow would be raised, probably the left one. My suspicion was confirmed when I looked up at her.

She was standing in the hallway and studying me with her head tilted inquisitively. When I caught her eye, the question on her mind seemed to change, and she exchanged my look with pure fire. She was waiting for me now that we were out of the sights of prying eyes, and I knew I wasn't the only one who had been tormented by the memories of our tryst. There was immense pressure on me to make my move. I couldn't let her down.

And yet somehow, the courage that had spurned me forward at the display case was gone. I was frozen. A panic began to settle over me. What was I supposed to do now? Try to meet the high expectations of the most dedicated perfectionist I had ever met? Was there anything more terrifying than trying to measure up to North's standards?

North seemed to have been anticipating my breakdown, because she sighed good-naturedly.

"Finch?"

"Hmm?"

"Come here."

Her words brought life back into my limbs and suddenly I was able to move again. She pursed her lips at me before turning her back and heading toward the bedroom, with me trailing numbly behind. This time I didn't stop to gawk at the expensive artwork framed on the walls. My eyes were burning a hole in North's back, and I wasn't going to let her out of my sight.

When I crossed the threshold into her room, she faced me and paused. I expected her to say something sarcastic and Northesque, berating me for not having the courage to make my move. To my surprise, her hesitation was brief, and instead of speaking, she reached out to me. My body was immediately electrified by her touch.

I moaned involuntarily as her warm lips grazed mine, leaving my lower lip buzzing when she pulled away. I gripped her chin, hoping to steer her mouth back to mine, but she resisted. Instead, her hands directed me firmly to the bed.

I toppled to my back and gasped as North climbed on top of me, somehow still able to straddle me despite her tight black skirt. Her skilled fingers were roaming my body, settling on my breasts as she buried her mouth into my neck. Hot tendrils of ecstasy coursed through me, and I lost all ability to speak. All I could do was feel.

"Do you remember what you told me the first time you came here?" North whispered into my ear. Her breath sent fire down my spine and I shook my head, whimpering helplessly as a new flood of desire paralyzed me beneath her.

"I'll never forget it," she said, keeping me in suspense as she slowly began to push my T-shirt up and stroke my abdomen. She traced a line from my belly button to my rib cage, and my hips bucked involuntarily as her long fingers left a trail of fire in their wake. "It was the first time anybody ever made me feel so…hot."

I was snapped out of my pleasure by a pang of self-doubt. Nobody had ever gotten North hot? That was hard to believe. But my dubious nature was soon forgotten as North's mouth found its way from my neck to the hard mound of my nipple. She gave it a gentle tug through my bra and I gasped, forgetting there had ever been any thought in my head but this beautiful woman.

"There was a point during the night when you told me something, lying right where you're lying right now," North continued, slipping her arm behind my back and expertly unhooking the clasp of my bra. "About just how much you love to lose control."

North's hot lips enveloped my earlobe and I moaned deeply. Suddenly my shirt was being pulled over my head and North had me pinned to her bed, the heat of her middle creating a delicious friction against my abdomen. She moved swiftly, her luscious lips suddenly wrapped around my bare breast. I gasped as she dropped North-scented kisses all over my body.

I reached out to try to strip her, but she gently brushed my hand away. I left her alone, realizing that she must not want to face the physical wounds that had been left by her attackers.

Instead, she focused her attention on stripping me, and buried her head between my legs, her tongue caressing me with long, delicate strokes. I had no idea that anybody could move so fast. I had barely registered the fact that she'd been strong enough to tug my jeans off. I gasped from the unexpected pressure of her mouth, and North reached a hand up to roam the curves of my abdomen, finally settling on the firmness of my hips.

It seemed impossible that she'd never done this with anyone before. Her every move seemed just like she was—perfect, calculated, and wildly successful.

A sudden explosion of bliss rocked me as her long fingers disappeared inside of me. I tried to keep myself from shouting out loud, but I couldn't stop myself.

"Fuck!"

It seemed to be just what she wanted to hear. I could hear a muffled chuckle as North's agile body rose and fell enthusiastically, matching the rolling waves of desire that kept my body tense against her sheets. If she was determined to succeed at being the best lover I'd ever had, her usual aplomb got the job done.

I could have surrendered to the pressure building inside of me at any point, but for some reason I forced myself to avoid my orgasm, again and again. Maybe I was afraid that if it happened too quickly, things would go back to the way they were, and I might never have another chance with North. Everything was simple in the moment, despite how complicated it could get, and I wanted to keep it that way. I wanted to relish her.

She caught on to my game, though, and I was startled to suddenly hear her voice.

"Finch," North said, her piercing eyes peeking up at me from below my navel. She was grinning but breathless and raised her perfect eyebrow at me before disappearing with a low moan that reverberated me from the inside out.

Between her phone call and my body writhing on her silken sheets, I learned one thing that night. You come when North Acquati tells you to.

CHAPTER TWENTY

It was strange being at Acquati Technologies the next day, being one of only two people to know the disturbing truth that North was trying desperately to keep quiet. Nobody else had a clue that the building had been invaded and North's office completely destroyed. It was our terrible secret.

We put the pieces back together before anybody found out about it, but I couldn't shake the eerie feeling it gave me to walk around with such dark memories. Especially when my coworkers were oblivious, going about their days as if nothing was different about the place. The reality of their job security being threatened would have been pretty sobering for most of them, whether or not they cared about North's safety. I felt like a traitor keeping something so huge to myself.

My apprehension wasn't made any better when I got to my office and realized that I'd left my USB in North's apartment, probably wedged somewhere between the headboard and the mattress. I couldn't believe what had happened between us. I'd stayed with her the entire night and woke up early just to watch her sleeping before we had to leave for work.

I gazed at the perfection of her face and studied the shallow breaths raising her chest. I noticed that she'd gotten up to change into pajamas at some point during the night, while I secretly relished in the feeling of her silk sheets caressing my naked skin. I smoothed the dark hair away from her face, completely sober now, and forced myself to face the thoughts that I had been so afraid of. I cared about North. A lot. I was attracted to her. I enjoyed sleeping with her. I wanted to spend time with her. Maybe even date her. And maybe, after a while, I could honestly say that I loved her. And yes, it was terrifying. But I wanted every morning to feel like this.

My face broke out into a hot flush of embarrassment when North's caramel-colored eyes fluttered open and she smiled sleepily at me.

"What are you looking at, Finch?"

"You," I said, pulling my hand away from her face and letting it settle in my lap. "I'm sorry."

"No," she said, sitting up and yawning. "It's time to get ready. I shouldn't have slept so late."

"You needed it," I said. She had exhausted herself in typical North-like fashion, outdoing herself again and again as she explored every crevice of my body. Her eyes flashed as if she were able to read my thoughts and she gave me a knowing look that deepened the red on my cheeks.

"Well, anyway, we should get going," she said. "Do you want to ride with me?"

North froze as she climbed out of bed and stretched. "Actually, that probably wouldn't be wise," she said before I had a chance to answer. "But then again, I'm sure that anyone who is trailing me knows who you are by now."

"Probably," I said, finding myself nervous for my own safety for the first time. The reality of the danger I was in hadn't fazed me much the night before. Especially once liquid courage was on my side. But now I wasn't so sure I would be willing to lay my life down for North's secret project. It wasn't as if she was even letting me in on the details. Besides, she had a brother who could deal with everything. I was off the hook any time I decided to be.

When I looked again at North, I caught a tenderness in her eyes that she turned quickly to hide. It melted me from the inside out. How could I even consider abandoning her?

We had a brief conversation over breakfast about what to do before we left. We decided to risk it and ride to the office together. I would take a cab back to my apartment that evening, where Bilbo would undoubtedly be waiting impatiently for his breakfast.

North and I arrived at the office several hours before everybody else was scheduled to begin working. Still, there were a select few who chose to keep similar hours as North's, though it wasn't clear whether it was to impress her or to take advantage of her flexibility so they could spend more time with their families. The early birds were puttering about the building, acting like everything was normal. But when I walked into my office, I didn't feel safe until I gave the whole wide space a look over. If the attackers knew that I was involved with North in any way, they would be after me next.

When I switched my computer on, I was surprised to find a lag in the system. It was bizarre, especially with all the money that North spent on state-of-the-art technology. I checked and double-checked my connection, but when nothing appeared to be amiss, I felt the familiar itch of investigation taking over me.

I cracked my knuckles, a terrible habit that generally put me into the mindset for serious work, and began sifting through the company's database. I found myself using skills I'd forgotten I had to try to pinpoint the source of the delay. I knew it wasn't my machine—it was like new and I had just updated it. Something strange was going on.

Before long, my suspicions were confirmed. A breach.

I knew security wasn't really my job, but I was feeling vigilant after the attack on the office. Whoever had been after North would obviously try to break into Acquati's system. Why hadn't I thought to check sooner?

I sprang upon the splinter in the system quickly. A message was encoded, set up and ready to be dropped into North's inbox at precisely 3:15 p.m., right after her lunch break. It was the exact time she responded to her emails. I knew because lately, mine were usually answered first. Someone had been watching her closely.

I had to spend a few minutes longer than I wanted to before I could fully decrypt the message. I was rusty at hacking, and it made me feel a little bit ashamed of myself. It had been like second nature to decode things like this. I'd been getting better and better at it, too, until the moment my life changed and I decided I wanted to be Acquati Technologies material. That meant I had to clean up my act and stay out of trouble.

On my third try, a tiny thrill coursed through me when the letters on the screen began to form into something that made sense. I was finally victorious, and a few brief sentences flashed onto my screen. I frowned, reading and rereading them.

We know what you did, and you're not going to get away with it.
There will be justice for the people you've hurt.
Soon the world will know. We will stop you.

Hurt? Who could North have possibly hurt?

I was incredulous and set to work until I was able to pull up the time stamp and IP address of the computer that had planted the message in our system. When I saw who it was from, my frown deepened.

I was familiar with the hacktivist group that had infiltrated our servers. They called themselves the Poison Ivy League. The group was a collection of Ivy League hackers gone rogue. They were dedicated to using their collective intelligence to stop crimes against humanity. And they were very avid fact collectors. If they wanted justice from Acquati Technologies, they would have a very good reason.

"Finch!"

North's voice broke into my deep concentration and I flinched, clicking away from the message with my heart pounding. It brought me back to the days of living at home, having to hide everything I was doing from the prying eyes of my judgmental and overprotective parents. In fact, I'd done a little bit of undercover work for the Poison Ivys when I was in college as a way to rebel a little bit against my strict upbringing.

Using computers for the greater good had been a cathartic way to spend time. I'd always gotten the biggest thrill from knowing that I'd helped to bring down some seriously bad people. There had been at least one case that had received international attention, some guy who was committing fraud on a massive level and running for political office, and it was one I had solved myself.

Of course, no one knew it except the other Ivys. We were under the radar. Still, it was an experience I cherished. I'd helped justice be served when no one else could. How many other people could boast the same? I'd brought down the bad guys.

North wasn't one of them, was she?

"Jesus, I called you five times. What are you doing?"

My mouth went dry. What wasn't North telling me? Her face was exasperated, and I could tell she expected me to speak immediately.

"Nothing," I managed to reply. "I was just playing a game and lost myself."

"A *game*?" North exclaimed, not even trying to hide her disgust. She didn't have to say what she was thinking. I wasn't getting paid to play games.

"You know, to clear my head. Competitive solitaire," I said, turning the monitor to show her my half-finished game. "It helps me think when I'm stuck on something."

"Ah," she said, her face softening. She sat down in the chair across from my desk. "I use a jigsaw puzzle for that. What are you stuck on?"

The gentleness of her voice seemed contrived after reading the message from the Poison Ivys. There was something she wasn't telling me. Something bad. And now I was involved too.

"To be honest, I was thinking about giving the box back to you. You can give it to your brother. I don't think I should be involved anymore with that. I'll still work on the project, but you're right. It's too risky."

"Oh," North said, her beautiful face suddenly creased. "Of course. I'll retrieve it from you this evening."

"I don't have it with me."

"Fine. Then whenever you're ready."

North stood abruptly and left the room, letting the door fall shut behind her. I thought I saw her hesitate for a moment before finally stalking down the hallway.

I felt horrible, but I couldn't let her jerk me around and keep me in the dark. I wouldn't put my life on the line for a cause I didn't understand. I still felt reluctant to give up the box, but I had blurted the first thing I could think of when she pressured me to answer. And it felt right, somehow.

I closed the solitaire game and pulled my browser up, my fingers poised with the determination of a new challenge. It was hard to ignore the racing of my heart, and the same adrenaline rush that had gotten me hooked on coding animated me with a passion that I had almost forgotten. It was an intoxicating thrill, knowing that I held the world at my fingertips. Had North forgotten that she hired only the best? If she wasn't going to tell me what was going on, then I was just going to have to find out for myself.

CHAPTER TWENTY-ONE

The next week was uneventful, but the message I'd found had shaken me. My search had proved rather unsuccessful, but I was determined. I had to know more about what was going on, but ever since North had left my office in a huff, I wasn't sure what to do about it. I just couldn't bring myself to part with the box she had given me, either. It felt like the only clue I would ever have about who she really was.

North liked to stay late in her office, so by the time Friday rolled around, I decided to do the same. If I went up to see her, I could plant a bug I'd been working on somewhere in the office. Maybe it would help me get a hint about what she was really up to.

After I was convinced that everybody had gone from the building for the night, I snuck up the stairs to North's office and stood outside the doorway, listening. It made me feel like a total creep, especially after North had been attacked so brutally in the office not long ago. I made short work of it and, with shaking hands, I rapped on the door.

"What? Who's there?"

The panic in North's voice made me immediately feel guilty.

"It's Aria."

I could almost feel the heavy sigh she let out as the tension left her body.

"Finch. Come in."

I pushed the heavy door open and walked into the office. It was colder inside than the rest of the building. She'd apparently had the air conditioner running full blast without bothering to open the door to the office, probably for hours. I couldn't help but shiver.

"What is it?" North asked, looking up at me sharply. "Are you all right?"

"Me?" I asked, laughing nervously. "I'm perfect. I just wanted to see what you're up to."

North raised an eyebrow at me, her eyes skeptical as they slowly roamed my body, but a small smile creased her face. "Perfect…"

I found myself staring hard at the sexy lines of her lips, lost in the shallow dimples that formed as they stretched into a smile, and a forbidden surge of heat rocked my body. I had to look away. It had been a terrible idea to come there.

"Well…" I felt stupid under her gaze. Of course, I wasn't perfect. I was the furthest thing from it. Being there seemed to prove it.

"As for what I'm up to? Nothing different, Finch. Did you bring the box?"

I hesitated. Despite being brisk, North's voice sounded so sad, even though there was no trace of emotion on her face at all. Could she somehow sense a Judas in her midst? Her dark eyes glittered in the golden glow of her desk lamp, and for some reason I felt ashamed of myself. Why couldn't I just bring myself to trust her? We'd been vulnerable to each other in ways most people never dreamed of. Was it really so hard to believe she was a good person?

I sank into one of the guest chairs. "No. It's not at the office."

North sighed and pushed her chair away from her desk. I watched, my heart tremoring, as she lifted her arms into the air for a gratifying stretch. I stole a glance at her tight abdomen, longing for a simpler solution to the complex feelings this woman always managed to evoke in me.

Finally, North's long legs carried her around the desk so that she was facing me, her arms outstretched behind her to support her weight against the broad surface of her workspace.

"I should never have gotten you involved," North said. Her expression was impossible to read. "I don't blame you for your reservations. None of this has anything to do with you, and jeopardizing your safety was a very naive move on my part. I'll escort you home; I assume that's where you're keeping the box."

"You don't have to do that..." I said. "I just need to understand. What is it we're doing?"

The conversation was getting tired; I could tell it from North's expression. Why did I insist on going down the same worn-out road with her again and again?

Still, this time, I had a plan, and clenched the tiny bug between my thumb and index finger. I could plant it in the chair as I left. That should work.

"You know we can't talk about that," North said with a tired tilt of the head. "Especially not here."

"Well, there's got to be some way..."

North's delicate jaw locked in frustration and I looked away, reluctant to allow myself to become victim to her temper. We'd been in a good place for a while now, professionally and personally. At least it felt good. Maybe too good. I wasn't sure if I could stomach her disapproval at this point. Maybe that was why I was in her office so late. We hadn't exactly left on good terms. Was the bug just an excuse to see her? If so, I was unforgivably weak.

"You were right, Aria. And I was right. It's not wise to involve you any further. My family and I can take it from here. You're free to go. Unless, that is, you'd like to be relieved of your position?"

"Are you threatening me?" I exclaimed, fire igniting in my breast. "After everything we…Are you going to fire me?"

North's hands were suddenly on my shoulders, lightning fast, and I could smell the intoxicating blend of her perfume. The sudden sensation of her nearness made me dizzy, and I inhaled sharply as she held me pinned against my chair.

"If I could fire you, I would," North said, her full lips just inches from my own. "You're causing me a lot of grief right now. Do you know what a distraction this is?"

"Distraction *what* is? North—"

Her sweet lips were suddenly hot against mine and a muffled gasp of ecstasy escaped me. I couldn't help but close my eyes and let myself be carried away to the heavenly place North's body always took me. I reflexively brought my hand to her face, letting my fingers get tangled into her thick, dark hair. Their grip tightened as her silky tongue caressed my own, and her left hand fell from my shoulder and slowly trailed down my torso, leaving fire trailing along behind it, until it was firmly between my legs.

I was helpless against her touch as North pulled away from my lips and buried her head in the nape of my neck, sending deep thrills jolting through my body as she massaged my middle through my skirt. Her soft, sensual lips found their way to my earlobe, and her hot breath made me arch my back as she whispered, "I've wanted you all day."

I groaned as North's hands slowly dipped down into the folds of my skirt, until I could feel her fingers pressing firmly against the thin fabric separating my flesh from her fingertips. It was the only defense I had against her, and she was pushing through my barriers with ease, one by one.

"Fuck!" I whispered urgently as her fingers suddenly disappeared inside me. I looked up into North's beautiful face; she was smiling broadly, a familiar light in her eyes. She had me exactly where she wanted me, and I was no longer sure whether that was a good thing or a bad one. All I knew was that I was powerless.

"North…"

But my protest was cut off when I cried out as she thrust her fingers deeper. I couldn't convincingly stop her. My body was a rock-solid testament to what it was I really wanted, and she wasn't going to let me off the hook that easily.

North gripped my head with one hand as she devoured the sensitive zone of my neck, every little touch electrifying me. I was honestly surprised. I had defied her. I'd tried to betray her. And now, she was what? Rewarding me?

Or was this all about North, and what she wanted? Was it that she was just craving sex, or was it that she wanted something more? My compliance maybe?

Suspicion was hot on my mind, but as her long fingers curled inside of me, all logical thought began to fade and all I was left with was the power of my own desire. I let my arm drop for a moment, just long enough to secure the bug on the underside of the chair I was sitting in. Thank god I didn't drop it. One brush with North's stiletto would have annihilated it.

Every inch of me ached for release until she finally had enough of torturing me. I could hear the smile in her voice when her supple lips brushed against my earlobe again, and the hot rush of breath as she whispered, "Come."

My body, traitor that it was, fell for it, and I hissed in pleasure as I began to quake, contracting around North's fingers. She sighed, a sound of soft appreciation, and I gripped her firm biceps hard to brace myself against the power of my orgasm as it intensified.

I panted as North slowly and deliberately withdrew her hand from my middle and pulled away, examining her fingers briefly before smiling at me. I felt embarrassed, maybe even ashamed, as she looked at me like that. I had come here with a purpose and had completely lost sight of my goal. I hadn't been able to get any information from her like that. I would never be a ballbuster like North. And the harder I tried, the more impossible it would be.

"I've got a lot of work to do, Aria," North said, fixing a meaningful look on me.

She was dismissing me.

"Of course," I stammered, getting shakily to my feet. "Good night."

"Good night, Finch."

I left the office in a hurry, and spent the whole drive home replaying the scene.

Although I was ashamed of myself for being so quick to give in to North's advances, I was proud of one little fact.

I had planted the bug. And she had been none the wiser.

Soon, I would know exactly what North Acquati did behind closed doors.

CHAPTER TWENTY-TWO

"No, you know that's not what I meant."

A little thrill teased me at the sound of North's sexy, textured voice filling my ears through the headphones. It felt wrong that I could tap into her office right from my bedroom, but such was the power of technology. At the moment, it didn't feel like the worst thing I had ever done…

There was silence, and I realized that North must be on the phone. I would have to find a way to tap into her calls as well if I was ever going to get the whole story. But that would have to wait.

"Donnie, I'm telling you. She doesn't know anything. Don't worry."

I perked up now, knowing that the "she" North was referring to might very well be me, and realizing that she was speaking with her brother.

"No, you're not going anywhere near her. If you know what's good for you, then you're going to leave her alone."

The fierce protectiveness in North's voice warmed me suddenly, and I felt positive now that she was speaking about me. And not only that, but she was speaking in a way that proved she cared. Elation surged through me and I felt a small, involuntary smile spread across my lips.

"Of course I love her. And I know you and she have a complicated relationship, but that doesn't mean you have the right to intrude on her life like that! Don't you dare. It is how it is for a reason, remember?"

My stomach dropped. North loved someone? Someone Donnie knew? Now I wasn't quite so sure who they were talking about. Whoever it was, it wasn't me.

"Stop it. Don't say that about her! I don't care whether you and Ma like her or not. You know there is nobody in this world I care about more than I care about her. I love her more than anyone. I didn't say that! Donnie, if you don't shut up and listen, I'm hanging up and you won't hear from me again until Christmas."

Apparently, whoever it was that North loved more than anybody in the world was someone that Donnie didn't approve of. And Donnie didn't even know me. It felt like there were rocks in my stomach, and hot, involuntary tears sprang into my eyes.

Bilbo seemed to sense my distress, because he head-booped my wrist, and I found myself petting him absently as I listened to North and her brother squabble over the merits of this mystery woman, someone who clearly held North's heart captive.

"I swear to god. Do you want me to come over there and shut you up myself?"

How could I have been so stupid? Women like North didn't go around falling for tech geeks like me unless they could serve her somehow. She had someone else out there in the world, a woman who knew her family intimately. Well enough that they all had their own unique relationships and opinions of her.

Would someone like me ever meet North's family? The chances of that were laughable. I doubted I could even visit her on a whim if I wanted to, let alone get invited to a family dinner. The whole thing was ridiculous. And why the hell was I crying anyway? I had always known in the pit of my stomach that North was bad news. Apparently, it just hurt to have the evidence. She had lied when she'd told me she had never been with a woman before. And worse, I had been hoping…

"No, I'm not sure what to do about the box thing."

My attention snapped back to the conversation, to North's tired, annoyed voice as she spoke with her brother. Now they were definitely speaking about me. Maybe I would get my answers.

"Yeah, I trust her. She's kind of like putty in my hands at this point."

North let out a soft laugh, one that sounded both sweet and sinister at the same time. My blood pressure spiked, and suddenly the tears in my eyes stopped flowing. So, she thought she was so smart, did she? That she had it all figured out and I was just some obedient little patsy? Well, I had news for her. Everything she said was being recorded onto my computer, and once I was sure I had what I needed, it was going to be sent immediately to the Poison Ivys. They would know what to do with it. I'd be hearing about the Acquati Technologies scandal in the news for years to come once they brought her down. And I'd be behind all of it.

"I don't know. She believes the attack was random. I didn't tell her that part. No, I'm not going to either. She doesn't need to know. It would put her in more danger."

A confusing pang of loyalty brought a warm surge through my heart, and again I found myself angry at my suspicion of her. What if she truly was just trying to protect me? I wouldn't know which it was until I figured out what the hell was going on. But even if she did want to protect me, that didn't change the fact that I was being played. She had someone she loved more than anything already. And it wasn't me.

"All right, Donnie. That sounds good. Yeah, we don't want it falling into the wrong hands. But you can't make it obvious. This girl is smart. If she weren't, I wouldn't have hired her."

North was quiet for a few moments as Donnie spoke. He was clearly impassioned by something, and she sighed, a low, Northesque sigh that made me wish more than anything that I could just be done with the whole tiring situation once and for all. I was an emotional wreck. An emotional wreck whose life was in danger for a woman who would never love me. And I had stooped to spying on her because I just didn't know *why*.

"That may be for the best. I'll give you her address."

The statement was spoken so softly, so innocently, and yet it sent a chill through my body. North was giving away my personal information. What, so her brother could come and get the box himself? What the hell was going on?

I felt violated. Betrayed in a way I never had felt before. This woman was ruthless. She would do anything for her company. Including throwing me under the bus.

"No, don't hurt her. Christ, that's the last thing I need. Don't even come around when she's there. I'll let you know next time she's at work and you can get it then. Matt will help you."

So now she was having people break into my apartment. That was just great. Whatever was in that box must have held the key to bringing her company down. I had to find a way to open it and get the information out of it. And if I couldn't, I would have to find someone out there who could.

"Look, I have a lot of work to do now, Donnie. Just give me a call once you have the box, all right? We don't need to do this again until then. You exhaust me."

I heard the distinct click of North hanging up the phone, and another long, deep sigh escaped her lips.

North thought *she* was exhausted? That was nothing compared to what I was going through. I felt like I had been put through a grinder. Apparently, Donnie couldn't intrude on her real lover's life, but gathering a troop of men to break into my house was okay.

I tore the headphones off and threw them across the room, shutting my laptop down and storming into the living room, where the box was sitting out, right in plain sight, on my coffee table. They were going to try to take it away from me, but it wasn't going to work. Because I had a plan. And as god as my witness, North wasn't going to get the best of me. I would get my answers. And soon, my revenge.

CHAPTER TWENTY-THREE

"Can you help me out or not?" I asked impatiently.

Jerrod frowned and turned the box upside down. "Do you need it exact?"

"As exact as possible. And as soon as possible. I'll pay you triple what you'd normally charge," I said, hating to sound desperate. But there was a lot at stake. "I've got a good job now."

Jerrod jutted his thumb over his shoulder. "Weigh it over there then tell me what it says."

I sat the box on the little scale sitting on the table behind Jerrod's desk, reading the numbers out once they finally settled. He sighed heavily and pushed himself out of his swivel chair, groaning from the effort. I took a look at him, surprised by how much weight he had gained just since we had been in college together. He already hadn't been a little guy.

He caught me looking and glared. Jerrod was the type to always make you feel as if your presence was a burden to him, even if it had been his idea to hang out with you in the first place. But he was the best I knew at this sort of thing. I'd had no choice but to drive for the hour and a half to his little office and hope that he would be able to help me. I had tried calling, but he screened his calls and rarely answered, and there was no opportunity for voice mail at all.

"You know," Jerrod said, his voice condescending and impatient. "When the Order has me craft swords, they give me at least a month. That's *reasonable*. What you're asking is ridiculous. And I don't even know if I have enough tungsten…"

"The 'Order' isn't under a time crunch," I snapped, biting my tongue before I blurted out just how obnoxious it was that Jerrod took a group of middle-aged men running around with swords in period attire more seriously than he took my life-or-death situation. "The issue is very sensitive. I could be in danger."

Jerrod exhaled irritably, as if my concern for my life was nothing but a self-important tirade. He stood up. "You wait here. It should take me about an hour."

"Are you serious?" I asked, my temper dangerously close to exploding out onto the one guy who could help me. "You gave me all this grief for an hour of your time?"

"I had plans today," he said dismissively, heading toward the door and tucking North's box under his arm.

"No," I said quickly, panic welling in my breast. "You can't take the box with you. I'll give you the pictures. I wrote the dimensions on them already."

Jerrod sighed disgustedly. "All right."

I dug out the photos I had printed before leaving the apartment and handed them to him, taking the box away and clutching it tightly in my hands. If I was going to damn near die for this thing, there was no way I was going to let it be taken into a room where it would be exposed to extreme heat. And Jerrod.

"Do you happen to know how to get this thing open?" I asked.

Jerrod frowned. "I'm not a locksmith, for god's sake. I'm a blacksmith."

I cringed at his use of the word; it seemed outdated and pretentious coming from his lips.

"Right. Just thought I'd ask."

"You know, tungsten is one of the most brittle metals. You could probably just smash it open if you tried," Jerrod informed me. "You don't need to rely on me for everything. I thought women these days were supposed to be independent."

He exited briskly, and I was left alone gritting my teeth in Jerrod's small, cramped office. I had dreaded the idea of making the trip out to see him, and now I was remembering exactly why. The whole thing had been nothing but a huge pain in the ass. I had even called off work just to be sure that nobody would be breaking into my apartment that day. North may have been brilliant and rich, but she wasn't infallible. Unless she had 24/7 surveillance on my home, I was safe to come and go as I pleased.

My chest tightened. How did I know she didn't have that kind of surveillance on *my* home? She had been there herself. I would have to comb through my every possession or set up a frequency that might detect an alien feed before I would feel confident knowing that North hadn't invaded every single part of my life imaginable. The woman was a living nightmare.

But would she have really had a chance to leave a bug in my tiny apartment? Her being there at all had been a huge fluke that neither of us could have anticipated. Unless she had staged the robbery just on the off chance that I would take her in…

The thought made me feel sick, and a peculiar twinge of guilt gave me a pause. North hadn't wanted to come with me at all. She had been wounded and scared, and the feeling of having her so near to me had been bizarre, but oddly intimate. Despite her larger-than-life appearance, she had seemed comfortable in my dingy surroundings, and some little part of me had been toying with the idea that her presence there might be something I could start to look forward to.

My thoughts ran away with me, lingering on the overpowering memory of her body, soft and sensual against my own. I had lost myself completely to that woman. Even now, through all the pain and hatred, my body was awakened by the pleasure of her memory. What the hell was wrong with me? I was a glutton for punishment.

I must have been daydreaming about North much longer than I realized, because before long, Jerrod returned, his expression bored and impatient as usual, and thrust a box at me. I took it from him, marveling at the exquisite detail. The outside matched North's box almost exactly. It would be good enough to fool anybody who was trying to snatch it away from me.

"This is really good, Jerrod. I've got cash. Thank you."

Jerrod said nothing, only tilted his head at me, his arms folded across his chest as I dug through my purse. He snatched the money away once I offered it to him and then went directly back to his swivel chair to face his computer screen.

"You're welcome," he said finally, putting on a bulky pair of headphones.

Apparently, that was the end of the conversation, and so I left, hoping against hope that this replica might work. It wouldn't fool North, but it should fool Donnie. And hopefully that would buy me all the time I needed to find out just what in the hell was going on and why my life was on the line.

* * *

When I got back to my apartment, I sighed, wondering whether I wanted to make the men who were going to break into my apartment search for the box, to make it believable, or if I should leave it out in the open so they wouldn't go through my things. The last thing I wanted was my space violated by a couple of grubby prowlers, but if it had to happen, I could at least make it as painless as possible.

I settled for a compromise and tucked the decoy box in the top drawer of my desk. I covered it with a folder full of sentimental notes that Thom had written to me during the beginning of our courtship. I had kept them mostly because I didn't know what else to do with them. It would hurt his feelings to find that I had thrown them away.

Nobody had ever written love notes for me before, and I was flattered by it to some degree. At the same time, though, they had remained in that folder, untouched and unread since

I had first received them. And none of them, even after all that had happened, compared to the full-body elation I'd had when North had given me the box.

Once the decoy was hidden away, I retreated to the bedroom with the real box in hand and lay down on my bed, examining it quietly. My thumb glided over the cool metallic surface, my heart drumming in my chest as the memory of North's body against mine brought a forbidden thrill coursing through me. Why was it that even now, knowing that she wasn't really mine and never would be, my body didn't seem to know the difference?

I gazed across the room, at the place where my headphones had landed on the floor after my fit of fury the night before. A sudden, desperate need to hear North's voice again flooded me, and I jumped from the bed and seized them, booting up my computer with a deep, shaky breath.

When it was ready, I tapped into the feed in North's office, my hands trembling as I turned up the volume. I lay back in my bed, fondling the little box in my hands and listening to North's soft, steady breathing. It was soothing in a way; I hadn't seen her all day and I was craving her like an addict, no matter how furious she made me.

North was typing furiously, the clicks of her keyboard filling the space in her office as my attention homed in on her, each little sound and movement putting me more on edge. I wanted nothing to do with this viper of a woman, and yet I was hooked, a slave to the thrill of her and this intoxicating game. I wanted nothing more than to storm into her office and demand to know who the other woman was and what the hell I was risking my life for if it wasn't her heart. And yet, I couldn't.

North sighed suddenly, a gentle, lonely sound that made my heart ache. It was hard to reconcile these contradictory emotions I was feeling, so I closed my eyes and listened, trying my best to stay objective. I was in control. I could fight this. All I had to do was stay focused.

There was a squeaking of her chair and she let out a gentle groan. I could imagine her lithe, slender body stretching as she leaned backward, her soft, dark hair falling gently over the slope of her full breasts. And then she released another gentle moan as her body relaxed and she leaned forward, probably hunkering down in front of her work again. It was late. She was getting tired. And yet she was keeping at it.

"Ugh," North muttered. The chair groaned beneath her as she shifted, and a soft sigh electrified my body; it was almost the exact sound she had made in my ear during her last orgasm with me. I had no power over the electricity that crackled beneath my skin, awakening the heat I tried so hard to keep buried. She was like a poison, steadily coursing through my system until I was completely lost.

But I was alone. Safe and alone in my room, relishing in the sensual sighs of her breath as she worked. I set the box down on the bed beside me and relaxed against my pillow, my hand draped casually over my stomach. I closed my eyes and found myself lost as I listened to her, my fingers creeping slowly down my abdomen toward the temptation stirring in my loins. I could almost imagine that she was at her desk, feeling exactly the same way…

"Fuck it," North said suddenly. It jarred me out of the moment as she clattered loudly at her desk, pounding the keys of her office phone.

My cell suddenly chirped shrilly from my pocket, and my heart leapt to my throat.

I tore the headphones out of my ears and answered impulsively.

"Aria?"

A shrill burst of feedback cut into her voice and I gasped, slamming my laptop shut. The noise ended abruptly, and I cringed, thankful that she couldn't see my face.

"What the hell was that?" North demanded.

"I don't know, you called me!"

North considered this a moment, then sighed irritably.

"All right. Why weren't you at work?"

"I left the message with Sandra. I'm sick."

"I want to see you."

My heart surged, and an overpowering temptation to go to her nearly brought me to my feet. But I had to stay strong.

This woman was not my friend. I didn't know exactly what was going on yet, but I couldn't trust her. I couldn't let myself be vulnerable to her again.

"I don't feel well, North. It really wouldn't be a good time," I lied. The timing actually couldn't have been better. I doubted it was work she had on her mind any more than it was on mine. But I couldn't give in. "I probably won't be in tomorrow either…I don't want to get you sick."

She was quiet for a moment, as if digesting my refusal. As far as she knew, we had parted on good terms. Maybe it was strange to encounter anyone who wouldn't jump when she told them to jump.

"Are you all right?" North asked finally, her tone significantly softer now.

The concern in her voice almost sounded genuine, and I wanted more than anything to believe that it could be. But there was no telling with her. She was manipulative. I had no idea what to trust anymore.

"I'll be fine. I don't want to keep you," I said. "I know you have a lot of work to do. I'll catch up on my work at home, don't worry."

"I'm not worried about that," she said quietly. "Good night, Finch."

"Good night."

I hung up the phone in a daze, my heart pounding wildly. I had managed to keep myself under control and refuse her, though it was probably the hardest thing I had ever done. I just hoped she wasn't going to get suspicious. I would have to keep playing the role of the good patsy, at least until I had the information I needed, but being sick was a good excuse. Still, the feedback might have given me away. I wouldn't know until I saw her again.

Worse than my fear that she would discover my treachery was the nagging pain in my heart. I had no idea what her intentions were with me. Why would North summon me like that? What the hell was going on? Did she just want me to leave my apartment so her brother could come in and get her precious box back, or was there more to it than that?

I looked at the box, lying stupidly beside me with all its mystery and grandeur, and felt a surge of anger sweep through me. I grabbed it and stalked to the living room, pausing on my way to heft an oversized hammer from the toolbox in my closet.

Bilbo was lounging on his back on the couch, his eyes wide as he watched me lay the box down on the carpet and deal a heavy blow to it. He shot off as I slammed it again, and again, until the metal was in pieces at my feet.

The box had shattered almost like glass, and my mouth went dry as I knelt to brush the pieces away to reveal what was left.

My heart sank.

It was a block of wood, only slightly smaller than the original box itself had been. I picked it up in confusion and examined it closely. It looked like it was a puzzle of some kind. It was made of a solid chunk of redwood, and unbelievably beautiful. I turned it over in my hand again and again, my fingers tracing the strange designs and grooves. I shook my head in disbelief as the cruel irony finally struck me.

It was another box. The only way inside, beyond sawing it open, would be to solve the puzzle. I wasn't sure whether to laugh or to cry.

Leave it to North. My mathematically driven mind would be aghast to destroy a puzzle it had never even attempted, and she had probably been counting on that fact.

I shook my head, an exasperated smile sweeping across my face. I was going to get her for this.

CHAPTER TWENTY-FOUR

"Thom! What are you doing here?"

"I heard you were sick, so I thought I would come by and bring you soup."

Thom smiled at me, that lopsided grin that made him so hard to refuse, and I opened the door wide enough to let him in.

He thrust a thermos at me, and my heart melted, though I had to turn away to hide the expression on my face when I remembered North's caution to me about a man who cooked like Thom did. A black heart? Really?

"Where did you hear that I was sick?" I asked.

"Oh…I work with someone who comes and goes at Acquati Technologies. He's a tech guy. I asked if he knew you and wanted to see if he would be willing to give you a note from me. Thought it would be a funny surprise. But he said you haven't been at work in almost a week, so I got worried."

"A tech guy? Who?"

"Chris," Thom answered noncommittally, stepping into my living room and stooping down to pet Bilbo. Bilbo seemed unimpressed and slinked away, his rotund belly close to the floor.

"Ah, good old Chris," I said, a vague recollection of a face flashing in my mind. Still, how did Thom know Chris? Wasn't that kind of stalker-y? I frowned, considering the possibility that North wasn't the only person I should be careful with. What did I really know about Thom? What if he was involved in all of this somehow?

The thought of having yet another complication in my already overwhelming love life was too much. So far, he had been nothing but friendly and fun and accepting of me. Maybe this whole thing with North just had me being paranoid. I couldn't turn every single person in my life into a potential enemy. I felt like I was going insane.

"So how are you feeling?" Thom asked. "Are you contagious? I hope you're not, because I'm going to be doing that big work thing soon…"

"Work thing?"

"I get to travel a little bit to look at locations for the next firm to be set up. It's a pretty big honor, really."

"That does sound really cool," I said, sinking onto the couch and unscrewing the lid of the thermos to take a sip. "This is actually really good."

"What do you mean 'actually'?" Thom asked, his handsome brow creased.

Great. I had hurt his feelings. Leave it to me—and to North—for planting the thought in my head that Thom was a horrible cook with a shriveled soul.

"I…just thank you, is all," I said with a nervous laugh.

Thom nodded and sat down on the couch beside me.

"So, we haven't spoken since that night you pretty much ditched me at the restaurant. Or did you not notice that?"

I froze. Actually, I *hadn't* noticed that. I had been so caught up in my job and my confusing relationship with North that Thom had been the last thing on my mind. All he managed to do was complicate things.

And yet, the woman I had practically left him for had somebody else. I meant nothing to her. All of it had been just one manipulation after another. How would I ever be able to trust her again?

"I'm sorry." I sighed. "I've been really caught up with things at work…"

"Well, you're home this week," Thom said good-naturedly. "And you never answered my question. Are you contagious? How do you feel?"

I sighed and found myself leaning against Thom's broad shoulder.

"I'm feeling a little better with you here," I said, surprised at the sincerity in my voice. It was true. With Thom there with me, it didn't seem quite so hard to picture my life without North's toxic hold over it.

Thom was the one I had chosen before I had somehow found myself tangled up in her complicated games. He had represented a security that I might not otherwise be able to achieve on my own. Sure, I was happy being an independent woman with a life of my own in my crowded little apartment, but with Thom involved, I could pretend I had something that had always seemed impossible for me to grasp: a chance at normalcy.

"Good," Thom said, putting his arm around my shoulder and holding me close. "You know, stressing yourself out can make you super vulnerable to getting sick. Or prolong illnesses when you get them. It's best to take it easy."

Thom's light, fresh-smelling cologne put me instantly at ease, and I found myself gazing up at him, a small twinge of arousal awakening in me as I did so. He was so handsome. What was wrong with me? Why couldn't I just make the sensible choice and stick with the incredible man who clearly cared about me? Was I some sort of masochist?

"I'm not contagious," I said quietly, looking up at Thom. He held my gaze and raised his eyebrow.

"No?"

I shook my head. "I think you're right and most of it has just been stress…I have definitely been overdoing it lately."

"That makes sense," Thom said, breathing in deeply. "You do tend to be kind of a workaholic. That's why I didn't really think anything of it when I didn't hear from you."

I cringed. Should I tell him about North? How I had ditched him during our date to spend the night in her apartment, only to succumb to the sensual gratification of her long fingers and generous, velvet tongue? How would I ever be able to explain?

"Kiss me," I whispered, closing my eyes and trying to push away the electric tendrils of longing the memories of North awakened within me. None of that had been real. It was all just physical. North had a woman she loved somewhere out there, and it wasn't me. It would never be me.

"I thought you'd never ask," Thom said.

The warmth of his lips against mine melted me and the gentle pulsing of arousal grew into a small flame. It wasn't fast and instantaneous like it happened with North, but maybe that was a good thing. Maybe it was better that I could hold on to myself with him. Losing myself only seemed to be getting me into trouble. Far more trouble than I could handle.

When our lips parted, Thom looked at me strangely.

"Aria. Why are you crying?"

I was shocked by the question and reached up to my eyes. Sure enough, hot tears were streaming down my cheeks, and I closed my eyes, only one image on my mind: North. North kissing someone else, just as I was kissing Thom. North, with her tenacious, passionate heart reserved for somebody else.

"I think I just missed you," I lied, standing up from the couch and taking Thom's hand. "Come on. Let's go to my room."

CHAPTER TWENTY-FIVE

"Finch! Where the hell have you been? I was worried sick."

North's voice made me prickle, and I gazed at her from behind the screen of my computer, doing my best not to be swept away by the beauty that usually kept me so enrapt. Today, instead, I saw only her flaws. The way makeup was caked a little bit around her eyes, how she had a long, shallow scar that reached from under her ear nearly to her clavicle. She wasn't a perfect goddess who was infallible. She was just another human being; a cruel, twisted human being with a secret that I was going to expose if it killed me.

"I've been at home sick, North," I said as evenly as possible. "Sandra surely told you."

"Well, I know, but..."

She trailed off, and it was clear that both of us were thinking of the several unanswered calls and voice mail messages that she had left for me during my week away from Acquati Technologies. I had been careful only to respond via email, so North wouldn't be able to sense anything was wrong from my voice. Otherwise,

I ignored her efforts at communication completely, deleting the messages before I even had a chance to listen to them. It seemed to be the only way I would ever fully escape the power of her spell. And it was torture.

"I have all my work done. You don't have to worry about that."

"Damn it, Finch. Is that all you think I care about?"

I pursed my lips, biting my tongue before blurting out exactly what it was that I thought. What I thought was that all of this was just a big mindfuck of a game and she was going to have quite a laugh at my expense one of these days. Probably with the woman she truly loved. The thought made me sick.

But I had resolved to play along, to not let myself push her away in case she got suspicious. I had to pretend that I still felt about North as I had always had: awe-stricken by her beauty and dazzled by her accomplishments. She had made me feel inferior for so long that it seemed odd to see her like this so suddenly, as if she were simply a morally corrupt human being who held no appeal to me whatsoever.

"I don't know, North. I'm sorry. I'm still not feeling that great. The doctor said it's stress…"

Dr. Thom to be exact, but North didn't need to know that.

"God, Finch. I'm sorry."

North sank down into the chair across from my desk, a look of pure and utter defeat spreading across her face. If this was an act, it was a damn good one. I felt a twinge of remorse for lying to her, until I remembered the phone conversation again. Things weren't adding up. I wasn't the one with a reason to feel bad.

"Why are you sorry?" I asked dully, wondering if Donnie and his lackey were in my apartment right that moment, pawing through my things in search of North's box.

The real box was hidden under my desk, beside my feet. I had decided to take it with me wherever I went and had adopted the rather embarrassing habit of carrying a woman's handbag around. Most people wouldn't think anything of it, but anyone who actually knew me would find it odd.

"I never should have made you do any of this," North said, her tired brown eyes fixed on me. I tried to read her for any traces of insincerity but found none. "Nothing is worth your health…"

Her voice trailed off and I swallowed hard, a heavy pang of guilt suddenly sweeping over me, sending a wave of nausea to the pit of my stomach. I had feelings for this woman, whether she was a snake in the grass or not. And I had betrayed those feelings by acting on my instincts with Thom. It had felt safe and sure and comfortable at the time, but now, with North sitting across from me, her beautiful face racked with guilt and misery over my supposed health problems, all I could feel was a deep sense of shame.

"I'm going to be fine," I assured her. "It wasn't bad enough that I couldn't work, right? You don't have to worry about me."

"That's the thing, Aria," North said, fixing a serious look on me. "I do. Your well-being means more to me than I can…I care about you. A lot."

She looked down at her hands, as if she had said too much already and embarrassed herself.

I wanted so badly to believe her words, but this woman was not the type to be so candid about her feelings. There was no way she could possibly mean it. Could she? North would never stop being a mystery to me. Maybe I had misunderstood the conversation with Donnie somehow. What if the woman North loved was an ex, someone who was out of the picture now and I didn't have to worry about it? What if she really did care about me just as I cared about her? It didn't have to be love quite yet… did it?

But even if that were true, North had still lied when she had told me she had never been with a woman before. Whether she had lied to make me feel better about her sex life or not, a lie was a lie. And lies were a slippery slope. I had to be careful with her. I couldn't let my feelings get in the way of finding the truth.

"Don't worry," I said. "I can take care of myself. If you didn't think that was the case, you wouldn't have given the box to me in the first place, would you?"

North looked suddenly put on the spot, then an easy smile brightened her beautiful face.

"To be fair, Finch, I hardly knew you when I trusted that box with you. But you're right. There was something about you that I trusted. And I still trust that. You're going to do the right thing. You're the one who is going to make me a success."

She rose abruptly, and my breath caught in my throat as the whirlwind of supple curves and long legs strode toward the door of my office. My eyes followed her, secretly relishing the movement of her hips against the tight black fabric of her skirt, until the door closed softly behind her.

When she was gone, I sighed heavily and sank back against my chair.

That had gone a lot better than I had hoped. But I was going to have to be on my guard. She might have been concerned for my safety, but that wouldn't keep her from doing whatever it took to get the job done. Whatever the hell the job happened to be.

CHAPTER TWENTY-SIX

"You've been avoiding me."

I froze, electrified by the sound of North's voice. I couldn't see her; she was behind me as I struggled to put my briefcase and an armful of slippery folders in the back seat of my car. I thought everyone had gone for the night and that the parking lot was empty, but somehow, she had managed to sneak up on me.

"North..."

Before I had the chance to turn around to face her, I gasped, a sharp, startling jolt of pleasure crashing through my body. Her arms wrapped around my waist, and the sudden nearness of her body drove all thoughts from my head as her fingers roamed down my arms, lingering briefly on my thigh.

"I don't like being avoided, Aria," North said, her warm body pressed against me now. I could feel her breasts on my back as she leaned forward, tucking a strand of blond hair behind my ear so her lips could whisper into it. "Do you know what happens to people who keep me waiting?"

My voice caught in my throat, and I glanced over my shoulder. When I met her eyes, my mouth went dry. She was looking steadily at me, her gaze fierce and beautiful. I found myself once again in awe of the perfection of her features. It was such a stark contrast from the way I had perceived her earlier in my office; she had seemed so flawed when I could think of nothing but how little I meant to her. Why couldn't I make up my mind?

"North, not here…someone will see."

North's hands stilled as she whispered, her soft lips pressed against my ear as she spoke. "I can assure you, they won't." The warmth of her breath brought a soft moan to my lips, and I could feel her smiling as her fingers slowly worked against the final barrier of cloth between her touch and my body.

I hissed sharply as North succeeded with a small chuckle, her touch engulfing me in flame. She knew my body well enough by now to drive me to the edge of my self-control. And as much as I hated her—*feared* her—resisting was the last thing I wanted to do. I wanted her. Despite it all, I had missed her too.

I moaned, biting down on my hand as her fingers found their way inside me. My body trembled as I made one last excuse to resist.

"It's not safe."

The words sounded strange spoken out loud. It was exactly what I had been thinking ever since she had given me the box—especially after I had heard the truth of how fickle her feelings for me really were. I wasn't safe. I could never be safe with her.

North froze with a soft, deflated sigh, and made a move to retract her hand. Before I could stop myself, I caught her by the wrist. "No," I whispered. "Just be fast."

North's eyes flashed with longing. She bit gently down on my neck as she pushed her long fingers in deeper. I shuddered, my body completely at her mercy. She sucked the nape of my neck briefly before returning her lips to my ear.

"Nothing is safe, Aria."

I couldn't protest. I had no genuine desire to. And I hated myself for it.

North's free hand reached around to massage my breasts, and I groaned into the back seat of my car, tendrils of pleasure snaking their way through my body. I was completely helpless against her.

North's breath was starting to come in short bursts now. She let out a soft moan of appreciation when I bucked my hips against her hand. It was the first time I had noticed her loosen her grip over that steely control of hers, and somehow it was almost more than I could take.

She seemed to sense this and began to double her efforts, until I was all but crying as my body succumbed to the power of North's skilled hands.

"Shh, Aria," North cautioned, her voice soft, almost loving, in my ear. I was imagining it. I had to be.

And then, as quickly as it had begun, it was over, and North was backing away from me. She waited until I got to my feet, my entire body trembling, before directing a small, almost sheepish, smile at me.

"Whether you're sick or not," she said, eyeing me with an expression I found impossible to read. "You should at least call me."

North turned on her heel and disappeared back into the building without another word.

I gaped after her, my hands wrapped around my waist. What the hell?

I wanted to be furious at her, but I just couldn't. Even if I didn't know what I wanted, she still managed to find a way to give it to me. And now, after my body had felt the tender caress of another person, the rest of the night was going to make me feel very lonely. It was already starting to.

I sighed, climbing behind the steering wheel and turning the engine. At least I always had Bilbo.

CHAPTER TWENTY-SEVEN

I didn't have the courage to listen to the live feed coming from North's office for the next few days. Instead, I focused my attention on getting in touch with the Poison Ivys. I had been far too consumed with my work life (or was it my personal life?) to follow up on my first lead. They seemed to have a grudge against North. And although it seemed unlikely for them to be behind the brutal attack on her office, there was a high likelihood that what they knew might at least be able to explain it.

It took a while before anybody got back to me. It would have taken much longer if I hadn't already been a member during my college years. It had taken me nearly two hours to compose the email that I sent, asking for any and all information they had on Acquati Technologies.

I felt like I was doing something wrong. Something that not only betrayed North, but also myself. There was some small part of me that was painfully loyal to her. But it was a ridiculous feeling. And unwarranted. Because whether she knew how to get under my skin or not, she was the one with all the secrets.

She made sure that she had the power, no matter who it hurt. Just like the message from the Poison Ivys had said. She was hurting people. She was hurting *me*. And I wasn't going to take it anymore.

I felt a surge of elation when I finally checked my email and found a brief note.

Meet me at Graham's.

It was sealed with the Ivys' insignia, and my heart thudded dully in my chest. They wanted to speak to me in person. All my insecurities came out full force and I tapped my hand anxiously against my mouse. It was almost like setting up a date with another woman. The anti-North. After what had happened with her that week, it felt even more acutely like a betrayal.

But if she wasn't going to be honest with me about what was going on, what choice did I have?

I was able to decipher the meeting time by the time stamp. Everything the Ivys did, they did it with intention. If I couldn't figure that much out, they would easily deduce I wasn't worth their time.

I arrived at Graham's just a few minutes before eight. I glanced around the dingy establishment. It was a bar, formerly a sports pub and now a free-for-all dive. I could feel the heavy eyes of hungry-looking men from the booths on the far wall, and I kicked myself for not thinking to change after work. I was still wearing clothes that were fit to impress North Acquati, when I could easily have blended in with my jeans and a superhero T-shirt.

"Finch, Aria."

I was startled from my thoughts by the direct voice of a young man. He was standing behind me, and apparently knew exactly who I was, which wasn't surprising in the least. I turned to greet him with a simple nod. He had dark hair and a serious demeanor. He was wearing a brown leather jacket and carried a black messenger bag over one shoulder. His eyes rested on me suspiciously, as though perhaps I was an agent of North's and would be mining for information to bring his organization down.

"Why don't we go have a seat?"

I offered a light shrug and followed him to a corner booth, where he sat down and immediately folded his hands over the table. I leaned back, raising a brow expectantly.

"So, you know North."

I nodded.

"You *really* know North."

I froze, slowly taking in his meaning. I didn't speak. I would let him make his point.

"We've been watching every move she makes. You can help us."

My chest tightened, and I shook my head.

"No, that isn't how this is going to work," I said, immediately defensive of my "relationship" with North. Whatever it was. "You guys are going to help *me*."

"Well, that's bold."

Finally, the young man's face creased into a smile, and he offered me his hand. "My name is Clayton. It's nice to actually meet you, Finch. They talk about you like you're some kind of saint back at base."

I hesitated a moment before taking it, then crossed my arms over my chest and sat back in the booth to look squarely at Clayton. There was no way that was his real name. He looked more like a Dudley. "I need to know what she's done."

"Is this a personal call?" Clayton asked, his tone slightly mocking. I exhaled in disgust.

"If she's hurt people, then I should know about it. I may be able to keep it from happening again. But only if I know exactly what the hell is going on."

Clayton mulled this over for a moment. "Acquati Technologies needs to be brought down. That woman should be in prison."

North? In prison? I couldn't picture it. I didn't even want to try.

"Why do you think that?"

Clayton sighed heavily and pulled his messenger bag into his lap. He rummaged through it for a few moments, then slapped a piece of paper down in front of me. On it was a photo of North, standing at a counter in what looked to be a bank. She was surrounded by people who were so poverty-stricken that half of them weren't even wearing shoes.

In her hand was a huge stack of cash.

"What's this?" I asked, snatching the photo up to get a closer look. Something about it seemed off. The expression on North's face. I had never seen it before.

"This is Ms. Acquati securing a workforce by paying the government for slave labor. She intends to utilize the people of this nation to work practically free in order to run her business more efficiently. She's sacrificing their quality of life to save money."

"North?" I couldn't help but laugh in disbelief. "That goes against everything she stands for."

"Everything she *claims* to stand for," Clayton corrected. "Come on. I thought you'd be smarter than that." He dug out more papers. Documents full of confusing words that my brain didn't want to believe. Sweatshops. Child labor. Percentages of money that Acquati Technologies would apparently be saving by "branching out" to an undeveloped nation. I wanted to throw up.

"So, this is what she's been up to," I murmured, pinching the bridge of my nose tightly in an effort to ward away the painful headache that was threatening.

"I'm afraid so. We've got ample evidence. But no matter how often we try to leak it to the press, Acquati seems to be ten steps ahead of us. I don't know how she manages to thwart us. She probably bribes the journalists. Whatever the case may be, it's unethical. There's such a thing as the free press! Or at least there should be. She's in violation of so many civil rights I don't know how she sleeps at night."

I listened numbly as Clayton spoke. I knew there was more he wanted to say, but I couldn't stomach it. Not right in front of him. This was something I had to digest, slowly, and on my own. Finally, his words caught my attention.

"But maybe you can leak it, Aria. She would never suspect you."

My stomach dropped and I immediately shook my head. "I don't know about that."

I was already in enough danger with the box, whatever it was. Did the Ivys know about it too? Is that why they had decided to meet with me in person?

"Look, I know it seems scary. She has a lot of power. But I don't think you should be concerned. We can protect you."

I shook my head and stood up. "You mean you can try."

I took the folder that Clayton had brought with him and tucked it under my arm. "I'll think about it."

And with that, I left.

CHAPTER TWENTY-EIGHT

My mind was reeling when I returned to my apartment. The first thing I did was grab the wooden puzzle that North had somehow manufactured to hold her most treasured secrets. What was she hiding? Why couldn't I remember what she'd told me that night? Why hadn't she told me again when I was sober? She claimed it was for my own protection, but it was becoming more and more apparent that she was only concerned about herself.

Clayton had told me that she was a relative monster. That everything she stood for was a lie. She was exploiting people. When she told me that Acquati was "branching out," had she really meant that she was gaining more workers in an unethical way to maximize her capital? She wouldn't be the first businessperson in the world to do it, but it was difficult to wrap my head around it coming from someone who had taken such a strong stance on running an ethical place of business.

I toyed with the puzzle, my fingers nimbly moving around the surface of the smooth wood as I tried to figure out how it was supposed to function. It took about half an hour before I made any progress and heard a soft click as a wooden square clicked into place. It was a little bit like a Rubik's Cube, then.

With that in mind, I worked tirelessly at it for the next few hours, until I was frustrated enough that I wanted to smash it against the wall. I couldn't risk harming whatever might be inside, though. It was impossible to judge by the weight, and I couldn't hear anything sliding around as I tilted the box to examine it from all angles. She had me stumped. Maybe she had never really wanted my help after all. Maybe this was all just a distraction to keep me from finding out the truth.

I sat the puzzle down with a heavy sigh and headed to my desk. Old Reliable, as I liked to think of my clunky desktop, was humming peacefully. I sat down in front of the machine, my fingers itching to do something more productive than trying to solve a puzzle that was clearly out of my intellectual range. If she had only given it to me to keep me occupied, like a hamster on a wheel, I wasn't going to waste another second on it.

What I *could* try to do was hack into North's email. I knew Acquati Technologies' security like the back of my hand at this point. It would be easy for me to get access to her personal computer if nothing else. I had done an ethical no-no by copying over the permissions to my own beast of a desktop. At the time, I'd only done so to try to keep up and stay above and beyond my workload so that nothing could jeopardize my career at Acquati. Now, though, it seemed that I'd been acting in my own best interest without even knowing it. I'd be able to tap into their network from home with ease.

It took me a little while, mostly because I was half-crazy with the itch to get back to the stupid wooden puzzle, but after what seemed like an eternity I got in and went directly for North's email. I wasn't going to show her any mercy. Not after everything I'd dealt with. I'd leave no stone unturned until I got the information that I needed. What I did with that information, however, was going to be a little bit more difficult to decide. Of course I would have to do what was right. Still, I would be risking everything. Not only my career and my relationship with North, but maybe even my life. If she was procuring slave labor, there could be any number of powerful people who could either want to stop me or target me for my association with North. That much was clear already.

I blinked as my computer screen flashed for a moment to alert me that I had successfully broken into North's email account. I let out a sigh of surprise and elation, gripping my mouse with a trembling hand as I prepared myself to sift through her inbox. My mouth went suddenly dry. What was I going to find? Was it going to completely change everything I had thought of her?

I had to admit, there was still some small part of me that was holding out hope that maybe I was misunderstanding something. Hadn't she told me that I was going to hear some bad things about her soon, and not to believe them? How would she have known that if they weren't true?

As soon as I started checking her inbox, it became obvious just how she would have known it. I was shocked to see that for the past several months, she had been receiving encrypted emails just like the one I had intercepted and decoded. They had been harassing her. I was torn between a feeling of protective anger and righteous satisfaction. She was being held accountable for her awful deeds. If she really was responsible for them.

I shook my head, trying to force the doubts away. Just because we'd been intimate didn't mean she was a good person. In fact, the most toxic types of people could easily feign affection to get what they wanted. And it was clear from the start that she had wanted something from me. What she wanted, exactly, I still couldn't determine.

My frustration mounted as I continued scrolling through her emails, hoping for any hint of what that thing might be. It was unrevealing. I let out a groan of disappointment and continued scouring all of her folders. I even tried to hack into her deleted messages, but everything was pristine. Except for the messages from the Poison Ivys. I made a copy of everything in her inbox just to make sure I didn't miss anything and put it on a flash drive. I could look through everything on my own time later without being connected to Acquati's network. That would take some of the pressure off.

Just as I was about to give up hope and break my connection from the company's network, a new email alert popped up and my eyes widened. The subject line read: *Greetings from Malaysia.* Was that where North was in the picture that Clayton had shown me? I hesitated for a moment before opening it. Would she notice? More importantly, did it matter? This could be my only chance to figure out if the Poison Ivys had the whole story.

Greetings, Ms. Acquati.

Your support in this endeavor means the world to every true patriot of our great nation. Not everybody would agree, but work like this is vital to our economic foundation and always will be. Thank you for helping us to keep our country strong.

Sincerely,

A friend

I read the email a few times, but no matter how hard my brain tried to process it, I felt dumb. What kind of work were they talking about? Why was the whole thing so damn vague? Whatever North was doing in that bank—apparently a Malaysian bank—it didn't look like it was keeping the people around her strong in any way. If this was about hiring slave labor to take Acquati to the next level, then of course there would be people who thought that she was malicious. However, I hadn't considered the people out there who might think she was supporting an industry that was vital to an entire country's economy. It was a little mind-blowing.

"Mreowr."

I felt a little claw snag against the denim fabric of my jeans and found myself snapped back into reality.

"Thanks, buddy. We'll have dinner in a minute," I said, reaching my hand down to give Bilbo an absent stroke while I quickly copied the final email onto my flash drive. I set the email to "marked as unread" before closing out of the network. When I was finished, I stared at my desktop screen blankly as the weight of my task slowly began to sink in.

Before, I had been clouded by my emotions. I had been almost hoping for something awful to come to be because of how hurt I was by the idea of North loving somebody else and not giving a shit about invading my space if it meant that she was going to get her way. The difference between then and now was that there was still the possibility that I was wrong. It could still have been a misunderstanding.

The more I learned, however, about this "secret project" that she wouldn't tell me anything about, was that it was bigger and more dangerous than she ever would have told me, even at that dinner when it felt like I had found the first person alive who seemed to be transfixed by my authenticity. I had been too afraid to believe it was true and drank myself into a stupor just to turn off all the doubts in my head. North had been drinking too, of course, laughing and smiling more than I had ever seen before, asking me things about myself and giving me the preposterous notion that maybe we could genuinely be friends…

Cognitive dissonance, right? That defiant buzzing in my head was cognitive dissonance. It made me too scared to doubt the evidence I was being given that the woman I had been starting to fall for was actually a monster. Even now, I was forcing myself not to go down another path of wondering whether or not I was misunderstanding the content of the email from Malaysia. Who had sent it? It wasn't above my skillset to figure it out, unless they had some really advanced security set up. It would take me a while, though.

"MOW!"

The urgent prodding at my jeans began again and I stood up, smiling down at my very impatient, very chubby, very food-motivated companion. This could wait until after we'd eaten, which was fine by me. I had a lot to think about.

CHAPTER TWENTY-NINE

North squinted down at the paper in her hands, her full lips pursed thoughtfully.

"I have to admit, Finch, this isn't your best work."

She set the paper she was scrutinizing down onto my desk. I had been just finishing when she'd come in and it had taken no time before she'd gotten her hands on the doodle. I hadn't been able to focus on my work, wondering if I was unwittingly helping somebody commit a crime against humanity, so instead of turning on my computer, I'd done a drawing of a stick man chasing a horse for stealing his hot dog. Clearly it hadn't impressed North's sophisticated taste.

"Do horses even eat hot dogs?" she asked, making herself comfortable in the chair opposite my desk. "I think if anything, they would be part of the hot dog."

"It's an expression of my inner angst," I said.

"It's cannibalism," she replied flatly.

I smiled despite myself, hating my traitor of a brain for still producing serotonin for a woman who was probably working on putting children to work as we spoke. It was easy enough to make jokes if you didn't see the consequences of your actions on a daily basis.

"Tell me. What is it that's making you angst badly enough to express yourself artistically? And I use that term loosely."

I picked up the sketch, avoiding the intensity of North's prying brown eyes before I let myself believe that the concern in them was genuine.

"It's nothing. I was just being dramatic."

"I don't think you were."

I studied the drawing with fake intensity and heard a soft sigh from opposite my desk.

"This is a lot for you, Finch. I know it is. I'm sorry for that."

My grip on the paper tightened. What did she know about it, really?

She noticed my demeanor immediately and stood up, coming closer to me and leaning on the side of my desk to speak a little more intimately. I ignored the fluttering of my heart. She wasn't worth this. That was the whole problem.

"Finch, please look at me."

I obliged, bracing myself for the worst. All I saw was North, her beautiful face studying me, her expression gentle.

"I owe you an apology, for a lot of things. I shouldn't have proceeded with you after you told me you had a boyfriend."

I was startled out of my gloom for a moment. My eyes must have visibly widened, because North inhaled slightly and held her breath, almost as if she were afraid of my response.

"It was my choice," I mumbled. Thom had been understanding. Neither were expecting me to commit to them. More importantly, that was the least of my worries. North was still playing this like nothing had changed. It was probably better for me to do the same. I wouldn't want to rouse any suspicion from her. I needed to stay close to be able to get the information that I needed to expose her to the world, so she could take responsibility for the monstrous things she'd done.

If she had done them.

My mind just wouldn't accept it to be the truth until I'd seen the proof for myself. Clayton had given me a folder, but I hadn't been able to open it yet. Every time I looked at it, I felt sick to my stomach, like I was doing something wrong in buying in to the bad things that people wanted to believe about North. There was an irrational, but very prominent, part of me that just wouldn't let go of the hope that she was the woman I had initially believed her to be.

Regardless, I had heard her dismiss me myself. I had heard her talk about someone she loved more than anything, and I had learned that she had lied. I hadn't expected her to be faithful to me when we had never even officially started dating or anything, but there was no reason for her to lie. It felt like I was walking on a tightrope of misinformation with her. How could I trust any of what she told me?

"Come back to me, Aria. What are you thinking?"

Her voice, usually commanding, had a much softer tone to it now. Why couldn't this just be genuine? It would feel so unbelievably good if it was real.

"The boyfriend thing was a bit weird," I admitted. "We're not exclusive, though. At least, that's what he told me when I tried telling him about..."

"Have you talked to him about me?" North asked, her voice still gentle.

"He made it easy not to have to," I said, sighing as the weight of one of the burdens I didn't even realize I had been carrying began to lift from my shoulders. "I'd been acting weird and told him we needed to talk. He pieced it together himself and we've just been taking things slow."

North nodded. Was that pain in her face? Or disgust, maybe?

"He was really understanding about everything," I said quickly. "I don't really know what I should be doing."

"Well. I can't advise you on that," North said. "Just do what feels right to you. And know that I never intended to make your relationship complicated. You make it stupidly tempting to act on compulsion. Perhaps..."

She trailed off, her gaze wandering beyond me and fixing on something I couldn't see.

"Perhaps what?"

"Well. Perhaps it's best if we discontinue our little... whatever this is. I don't want to be responsible for making you feel this way."

Why my heart seized up in panic I don't know, but I do know my mouth replied before my brain could process what was happening. "No."

"No?" North raised her brow, the hint of a smile curling her lips. "And what of the black-hearted cat neglector?"

"I told you, we're not exclusive. I just have some things to figure out."

Like whether or not you're intentionally fucking with my head so I can unwittingly help you set up a company that runs on slave labor.

I didn't say the last part, and North's face lit up.

"Excellent. Then I didn't waste my time coming down here."

"What do you mean?"

"I was going to ask you if you wanted to join me tomorrow night on what one might consider a date."

I gaped at North, the words and their meaning not fully processing in my mind.

"A what?"

"A date. You know, where I take you out and be all impressive, try to sweep you off your feet...I don't think I'll let you drink this time, though."

"A date." The words felt funny in my mouth.

"Finch, I'm not going to say it again. If you're not interested that's perfectly fine. I thought it would be a nice change of pace from...well..." She glanced at the sketch. "Horses and hot dogs. You know."

I felt a sudden exhaustion that seemed to be radiating from the depth of my soul. If I went, I'd be putting myself at risk of being unable to deny my greatest temptation. If I didn't go, it could hurt my chances of staying close to North long enough to be able to expose her publicly once and for all.

With a deep inhale, I nodded. "Count me in."

"Great," North said, beaming. "You won't regret this."

She left the office in her usual brisk manner, completely oblivious of the fact that I already did.

CHAPTER THIRTY

"How was your flight?" I asked Thom, gripping the phone tightly between my cheek and my shoulder as I frantically looked through my closet. What in the hell was I going to wear? For the first time in my life, I was wishing I had listened more to my mother about buying clothes that were designed to impress. The closest I'd managed were my work clothes, and I wore those all the time. What was wrong with me? Why couldn't I "girl" right?

In all fairness, though, I hadn't expected to ever go out on an actual date with North. Why couldn't it have happened before I'd been disillusioned by her?

Probably because I had been so horrified by my attraction to her that I made an ass out of myself around her just about every chance I got. I should have gone shopping the second she'd asked me.

"It was good! Uneventful. Which, when traveling, is ideal."

"Good to hear," I said, trying to keep the strain out of my voice as I lifted a box of untouched clothes from the back of my closet. Maybe there would be something in there. Old gifts from my mom that I'd felt too guilty to throw away or something.

"How about you? You been staying out of trouble?"

I had to bite back the cruel bubble of laughter that welled in my chest. I was proud of myself when I succeeded.

"Nothing new over here," I said noncommittally. Still involved in a horrible scheme to help North build sweatshops. Still halfway wrapped around her little finger. Same old, same old.

"Good. Listen, the guys are here, and we have a few things to go over. You know. Work things. Can I call you later tonight?"

"You're a free man," I said, knowing full well that later that night I would probably be with North. My heart fluttered at the implications, and I had to physically shake my head to stop myself from being delusional. Nothing could happen between us. It wouldn't be real even if it did.

"Well, then, I'll talk to you later."

"Okay. Later, Thom."

We hung up and I set my phone down on my dresser so I could properly go through the box that I had managed to lug out of my closet.

It wasn't a huge shocker to find that I wasn't happy with a single article of clothing in it, and I seriously debated going out to buy something new. Was it really worth spending money on impressing North at this point, though? Obviously not. Instead, I decided to go with the dress that I'd worn the first time she'd taken me out. Even though it seemed like the single most pathetic thing I could ever do, it was possible that she wouldn't remember. I had only worn it around her once, unlike the other things in my closet. It would have to do. She could take me or leave me.

It seemed like there was a glitch in time, because the very second I had settled on the outfit and gotten myself ready, there was already a light knocking at my door. North had arrived.

I felt breathless for a moment, nearly on the verge of a panic attack. I managed to calm my nerves enough to answer the door, but when I did, my face fell in confusion. Not North. Her driver.

"Aria Finch?"

"Yes."

"Ms. Acquati wishes me to escort you to the limo."

"Limo?"

"Yes, ma'am. I believe she said something along the lines of giving you the full 'North Acquati experience.'"

His voice was dry, almost a monotone, but his eyes sparkled. It seemed her sense of humor wasn't lost on him. I, however, was ready to bolt back into my bedroom and call the whole thing off.

"Are you ready? Ms. Acquati doesn't like to be left waiting."

I nodded dumbly and the driver beamed at me as he led me outside to where the limo was parked. I couldn't see any sign of North behind the tinted windows. The driver opened the door, silently inviting me to duck inside.

When I did, I was hit powerfully by North's signature scent, and she caught my eye, smiling broadly.

"Good evening, Aria."

"Hey," I said, feeling suddenly stupid in my choice of dress. She was looking dazzling, as always, in a formfitting red dress and heels to match. She was wearing a crystal necklace that once again reminded me of how easily I'd be able to get rid of my car payments if our positions were switched. She was beautiful. North couldn't afford not to be seen in designer clothing. I, on the other hand, had a collection of T-shirts with different comic book sound effects printed on them.

I might have looked mediocre, but, on the plus side, I hadn't decided to wear one of *those* tonight.

"I thought we could try and have a normal night together for once. You know what they say…live each day like it's your last."

I paused, the words not sitting well with me.

"Oh, don't be alarmed, Finch. I only mean that if today were my last day, I think I'd regret not asking you out with me."

"That's still a little bit cryptic," I replied, eyeing North thoughtfully. It appeared that death was on her mind. She'd already been attacked for whatever mess she was making for herself. Maybe it was genuine. Or maybe she was just trying to get me out of the house so that her goons could steal what they thought was the real box. Either way, I had it in the safest place I could think of. Even if they realized the box that I'd planted was fake, they wouldn't find the real one.

"I'm sorry. I was going for romantic." She looked flustered for a moment. "Guess I need some practice."

Then she smiled at me, an easy expression so infectious that I couldn't help but smile back.

"So," I said, clasping my hands together tightly. I had a feeling that if I didn't, they would start shaking. It was strange to be in her limo like this, knowing that her intentions for the night were romantic. We had never done anything to be specifically romantic before, and I had no idea what to feel about it. I might have celebrated just a few weeks ago. Why did everything have to be so messed up? "What do you have in store for me tonight?"

This got her brown eyes twinkling and she shook her head slightly. "It's a surprise."

"Oh...okay."

"Relax, Finch," she said, taking my hands into hers. They were warm and comforting, even though she was what had me on edge. "I'll take good care of you."

I nodded, doing my best not to let my misery show on my face. She squeezed my hands and then released them, seeming to sense my resistance to her. She didn't let it deter her, though. She was probably used to my fickle temperament.

"I sent you a gift. Did you receive it?"

A gift?

"No. Another box?"

North's eyes hardened and she looked to window separating us from the driver.

"Did you forget to call in the flowers, ya jerk?"

I froze, not knowing how to respond to North berating her driver.

"Ah hell," the driver mumbled. "I told you to remind me after the game, North. Sorry."

North muttered what I assumed to be some Italian profanity under her breath. "No, it's my fault. I should have done it myself."

"Flowers are old-fashioned anyway. You remember what Grams used to say?"

"I'm closing the window now," North said warningly. Her slender finger found a button I hadn't noticed before, and soon we were in a silent bubble.

She sighed and lifted her shoulders in a slight shrug. "I've been busy. We all have. There were supposed to be flowers."

"It's okay," I said, rushing, for whatever reason, to reassure her that I didn't need flowers. "Is that your brother? Donnie?"

North shook her head curtly. "No. That's my cousin Matt. He promised my parents he'd keep me safe, so he volunteered to be something of a bodyguard. Don't worry, though. He's paid handsomely for the privilege."

She flashed me a bright smile, obviously eager to change the subject. Their little discourse appeared to have embarrassed her a little bit. It was almost cute.

"It's nice that he cares about you," I said. I meant it. It was also nice that she had made sure her cousin had a well-paying job. She had always seemed like the kind of woman to remain faithful to her loyalties and take care of those closest to her. Too bad I knew better, now.

"Oh, you can't stop my family. They're smothering," she said, grinning. "I suppose it's nice. I'm lucky that way. We drive each other crazy, though."

I remembered North's parting words to her brother on the phone the night I had been listening in to her conversation in her office. If he didn't shut up, she wouldn't talk to him again until Christmas.

"We don't have to talk about family things," North said quickly, seeming to sense the shift in my mood. "I know they're not the most exciting thing in the world."

"No, I don't mind hearing about your family." I just wished I knew what to believe.

"Well, let's change the subject anyway, shall we?" North thought for a moment. "If you could go anywhere in the world, where would you go?"

"Anywhere?"

"Anywhere."

"That's hard to say…" I paused to think about it for a moment. For the longest time it had been my dream to work at North's company. I was going to have to come up with a new dream soon. If I was able to expose her, that would ruin my career. "Maybe in Europe somewhere."

"Europe, you say?"

I nodded. "I've never even been out of the country. Just moving to Chicago was a huge deal for me."

"Where are you from originally?" North asked.

"Indiana. Hammond."

"Fancy."

"Not quite."

North grinned. "I'm from northern Italy. Lecco."

"Lecco?"

North nodded, and I took my phone out of my pocket, quickly absorbing myself in it.

"Finch."

"Hmm?" I asked, without looking up.

"Please stop researching my hometown."

I snorted. "It's hardly a town. Look how beautiful it is." I shoved my phone at her, forcing her to look at the sweeping hills and rich architecture. "Why would you ever want to leave? Why come here?"

North grew quiet for a moment. "It seemed the place with the most opportunity for me."

"Look at the mountains!"

North smiled at me, a tenderness in her expression. "Maybe you'd like to visit there someday. When you go to Europe."

"Absolutely."

How she had managed to get me out of my head long enough to forget that she was supposed to be my enemy, I don't know. It was easy to lose track of anything but the present moment with her. Despite my anxiety, I felt comfortable with her. Peaceful. Happy.

I couldn't let myself get lost in that. I had to stay realistic. Remember the goal—and the stakes.

We came to a stop and the engine cut off. I heard the driver, or, more precisely, North's cousin, get out and round the limo. A few moments later, the door opened, and he smiled in at us.

"Your jet is ready for you, Ms. Acquati."

"Wonderful. Let's move, Finch. I'm about to show you the world."

CHAPTER THIRTY-ONE

North's heels clicked purposefully in front of me as she pulled me down a huge, gray expanse of pavement. My mouth was completely dry at this point. She was taking me on a *jet*? Where would we go? What if she'd found out that I'd breached her email and was going to get rid of me and dump my body somewhere?

"A jet?" I managed.

"I wanted to show off a little," North admitted, her brown eyes clear and bright. "Sue me."

"I didn't know we were going to fly."

"Don't worry so much, Finch. My pilot is one of the best there is. There are accommodations on the plane. You'll be perfectly safe. I've done this a thousand times."

I swallowed hard. North's cheerful demeanor didn't falter, but she did take my hand and squeeze it reassuringly. "Come on. That's a girl."

She helped me up the steep steps and into the cabin. It was a ridiculous level of luxury. Everything was a bright white, just like in her apartment. She showed me where we would be sitting for takeoff and again took my hand in hers once we were seated. She could tell I was terrified.

"If this is too much, you don't have to do it," North said. "We could go somewhere else. Are you all right?"

I nodded quickly. "I'm fine," I said. "Is there water?"

North smiled warmly and nodded. "There is. And the, uh… lavatories…are back there."

She pointed in the back to a small room, and some random, stupid joke about the mile-high club popped into my head. I might have made it if I could think straight. Instead, I took the water that someone on North's staff had mysteriously provided for me and drank deeply. Unsurprisingly, it didn't exactly soothe my nerves. Still, the dryness in my throat was temporarily taken care of.

North's staff disappeared from view as the engine turned and we slowly began to creep forward for takeoff. I could feel North watching me closely and I tried to keep my gaze forward.

"Have you ever flown before?"

I shook my head. "I drove myself and my things from Hammond."

"Ah…well, you're in good hands."

I didn't doubt that North could afford the best pilots available, but I still wasn't sure about the purpose of the trip. If she wanted to get rid of me for everything, it would be very easy. She wasn't a murderer, though. She couldn't be. Her driver, on the other hand…who could say? He was up in the pilot's cabin now.

"You have a passport, correct?"

I looked up sharply at North. Just what was she planning?

"Yeah," I replied. "It was one of your requirements upon hire, remember?"

"Did you bring it?"

"I wasn't planning on leaving the country today."

North smiled. "That's all right. We'll just be going to New York for now."

"New York?"

North beamed. "I haven't had time to cook lately, but I wanted you to know what genuinely good lasagna tastes like."

I couldn't help but laugh. "You're competing, aren't you?"

"What, with your 'boyfriend'?" She spit the word out dismissively with a tired wave of the hand. "I don't have to try very hard to compete with him. You're here, aren't you?"

"Well…yeah," I mumbled.

"By choice, correct?"

I squirmed. "Yeah…"

"You chose to come on to me at the restaurant during the company dinner. You chose to tell me you wanted to see where I live. You chose to say yes to my attention, my affection. You practically discarded the poor boy, and now you're telling me I'm competing with him over his shitty lasagna?"

I couldn't tell if she was angry or just teasing me, so all I could do was nod meekly.

"Am I winning?"

I laughed despite myself. Why was this so difficult? I cursed myself for being stupid enough to drink so much the night she had revealed her plan to me. It was my own fault I couldn't remember what she had told me, but if she wasn't planning on changing her story to suit herself, then why wouldn't she just tell me what was going on?

"I enjoy your company, Aria. A lot," North stated, her tone firm. "I don't understand why that's so difficult for you to accept. I'm not just some corporate goon with no heart. I like you. I care about you."

She sighed, leaning back in her seat and crossing her hands over her stomach. My head was swirling as my mind struggled to take in the words. I had been afraid to admit that I wanted to hear them from her.

What the hell kind of timing was this, though? She couldn't possibly mean it. Then again, if she really did plan on killing me, maybe this was a mercy. Tell me all the sweet things so that my last few hours would end up being tolerable.

"North, I…"

She held up a hand. "It's all right, Finch. You don't have to say anything. I just want you to have a good time. No pressure from me about anything. Today is about lasagna."

She flashed me a dazzling grin that put an end to the matter and the jet jolted forward. My stomach lurched and I looked around the cabin in a panic.

"Um…Aria?"

"Hmm?"

"Are you going to vomit?"

I shook my head quickly, though that didn't do much to help my nausea.

"Drink your water and sit tight. I've got peppermints in that little compartment there."

She gestured to a fixed area secured between our seats and I dug around for one, closing my eyes in relief, and to block out the sensory input of the jet's launch into orbit.

I heard North chuckle. "This is off to a rocky start," she mumbled just before lacing her fingers through mine. Despite my reservations, I let her touch comfort me as we lifted off.

CHAPTER THIRTY-TWO

The jet trip took about two hours, and North entertained herself by asking me twenty-one million questions. She managed to find out about the dog that I'd had in first grade, the way kids in school used to call me Geeky the Motherboard Slayer, and even the fact that I'd worn jeans to my prom and left early because of how much I hated the music.

"How did you manage to get away with wearing jeans to a formal?" North asked, apparently impressed by the feat.

"The computer teacher was one of the chaperones, and he knew if they didn't let me in, I would quit tutoring the other kids."

North grinned. "I don't mean how you made it into the school. How did you get past your *mother*?"

I burst out laughing. "She didn't see me leave. I'd been so horrified by all the preparations she had been making for me that I snuck out the window and met my date at the pizza place."

"Lucky guy," North teased.

"Not really, I left early."

"Without your date?"

"Well, yeah. What if he wanted to…well, you know?"

North peered at me. She knew.

"You didn't."

I shook my head. "I went home and played video games."

North snorted. I looked at her, startled. I was unaware that she was capable of making that sound. All it did was dissolve us both into laughter.

When we finally landed, I wasn't quite so concerned about the turbulence as I had been on the way up, but again, I found my hand in North's until we were settled at a stop and it was safe to stand.

"Well, Aria, how did you like your first flight on a private jet?"

I smiled. "It wasn't bad at all."

North beamed. "Excellent. Come along now. There's lots to be done."

We bustled from the jet to an awaiting vehicle, and again I tried not to think about how much money all of these things represented. If she was trying to impress me like she'd said, she was doing a good job. What was I supposed to do with myself, though? I had never had money like this before in my life, and knowing that North did, and that she could do just about whatever she wanted with it, was a bit terrifying.

"I've been looking forward to this since you said yes. I'm famished," North said, holding the door to the back seat of the car open for me so I could get inside. She sat down beside me and sighed contentedly. "You're not going to forget this. And if you do, I will be personally insulted."

I nodded, still not really sure what was in store. Something about lasagna, right? But why did we have to go all the way to New York City for lasagna? Did they have some fancy, upscale, fine-dining experience that no one would ever be able to afford unless they were a gorgeous billionaire who was trying to make my last moments on Earth somehow more comfortable? Big windows and sparkly chandeliers and rectangular plates with three tiny morsels on them…

I found out soon enough. After about forty-five minutes on the road, we pulled up to a brick duplex. As soon as North opened the car door and we stepped outside, I could smell the scent of spices wafting through the air. I peeked at North, who was gazing at the building, a wistful smile playing at her lips.

"Let's go, Finch."

She laced her arm through mine and led me to the door. She rapped on it a few times and we waited for a moment before a plump little Italian woman with gray hair opened it and let out a loud exclamation. She threw her arms open, and North released me to embrace her.

"Hi, Nonna!" They hugged and chatted in Italian for a moment before North appeared to remember that I was there. "Aria, this is my grandmother, Eleonora."

The little woman shook her head enthusiastically. "Nonna!"

"Yes. My nonna."

I smiled. "It's nice to meet you," I said. The little woman nodded and gestured for us to get inside. The house smelled heavenly, and I soon found myself sitting on a comfortably worn-in couch much like my own. I felt far more comfortable here than I had in North's apartment.

"We going to feed you!" Nonna exclaimed. "And you will learn what love taste like."

I shot a look to North, my eyes narrowed.

"*You told her?*" I whispered severely.

North gave me a light, unapologetic shrug. "I wanted to make sure she wouldn't say no. Ever since I ate that atrocity, I've wanted Nonna's cooking. It's the best way to wash away the taste of a bad meal."

"You're horrible."

North laughed with genuine delight before joining her grandmother in the kitchen. "Wait here, Finch. Nonna did all the hard parts, but I'm going to help with the rest."

"Uh…okay."

I was left alone in the living room, wondering whether or not a poisoned lasagna might be part of the master plan. But listening to North and Nonna giggling and speaking rapidly in the kitchen soothed my fears. This was just a family. They were happy to see each other. And, North had promised me lasagna.

I sat alone in the living room, looking around at the furnishings. Photos of strong-featured people who I presumed were part of North's lineage lined the walls, and I grinned when I noticed a picture frame on Nonna's mantel. It was a magazine cover with North's grinning face on it. Close by was a photo of two little girls, identical in everything but their outfits. North and her sister. It had to be. I tried to figure out who was who until the meal was ready. North came out of the kitchen like a vision from a dream, her beautiful face more serene and at peace than I had ever seen it.

"Dinner is served," she said, her tone quiet. I looked at her for a few moments, unable to speak or think or feel. All I could do was see her.

She seemed to sense that I was frozen in place, because she walked over to me and offered a hand to help me up. "I can get lost in this old couch," she said with a laugh. "Come on. Nonna's eager for you to eat her love."

We were both laughing as we sat down at the table and I feasted on the most delicious lasagna I had ever tasted. Half of what North and her grandmother said was in Italian and went over my head, but I didn't mind. It felt like home, and for the first time since all of the bullshit had started, I took North's advice and relaxed.

CHAPTER THIRTY-THREE

"Nonna likes you," North said, waddling to the car beside me, patting her full stomach contentedly. I had never seen a woman eat the way North did and still maintain such an incredible figure. Either she was naturally blessed with a lightning-fast metabolism, or she approached her body maintenance the way she approached her work.

"I like her too," I replied, smiling. "She's sweet."

"That's what she said about you," North said, looking at me with twinkling eyes. "Well, after I told her that about you. Then she made her mind up for herself."

"I can't believe you talk about me to your grandmother," I said, laughing.

"What can I say? You're on my mind a lot."

Now there was something that I could relate to.

"Back to the car, Finch. We have one more thing to do tonight before it gets too late."

"What's that?"

North flashed me a killer smile and I almost forgot what we were talking about. "Shopping, of course."

I shook my head.

"I didn't bring very much money with me," I protested.

"You're misunderstanding. *I* am taking *you* shopping. If you don't want to consider it charity or a date trying to spoil a beautiful woman, then think of it as an investment so you can look good enough to represent my brand. I will use the company credit card and get a tax write-off for it. Everybody wins."

Except the slave laborers, obviously.

North's brow furrowed for a moment. I must have looked as distressed as I felt. "If you really don't want to go, we don't have to."

"It's not that," I said.

"Well, maybe someday I'll figure out what's going on in your head, Finch," North said. "Come on. I want you to see the sights before we go."

I nodded, and soon I was being whisked into the epicenter of the city.

* * *

I don't know how it happened, but North managed to cajole me into spending a painful amount of money on designer clothing. It seemed to make her happy, and to be honest, after the fiasco with my closet earlier that day, I was more willing than normal to spice up my wardrobe a little bit. I couldn't believe the selection in the stores, and it was actually a lot of fun to just spend time with North and try on outfits. It was especially nice to see her eyebrows shoot up to the ceiling when we picked a winner, and the way she'd nod dumbly, pointing to the cart.

I couldn't help myself. It was nice to have a little taste of the luxury that North experienced every day. I felt guilty knowing that it was more likely than not blood money, but I was having such a good time that I willed myself not to think about any of the complicated things until I was safely back in my apartment. I wouldn't be able to hide the shift in my mood from North if I had one, and it felt good to be with her. I wanted to hold on to that, to make it last. It would come to an end soon enough, and the thought was enough to make me want to throw up.

"That went well," North said as we finished loading the bags into the car. It was late evening now, and she smiled warmly at me once we were tucked inside the back seat together. "I arranged a room for us, so you don't have to spend the rest of the night on the jet. Is that all right?"

"Oh! I…"

The implications began flashing in my mind and I bit back a surge of panic. I knew I should say no. She was giving me the option, watching me as she waited for the answer.

"I didn't expect that."

She leaned close to my ear, her breath hot on my skin. "I missed sleeping beside you."

My body exploded with an unwelcome want. All I could do was nod dumbly as the car zipped us through the streets of the city. We stopped in front of the biggest hotel I had ever seen. I was dazed by the lights, but not for long. Soon, North and I were being escorted through the building by the concierge. We took an extravagant elevator up to an even more extravagant room. Our shopping bags arrived not long after, and then it was just the two of us.

"Come here," North whispered, dimming the lights and grabbing my hand. She tugged me over to the big window and drew the curtains open. "This is the best view of the city you'll get in this building."

Sparkling lights danced before me like stars on the ground, sprawling endlessly into the night. The whole place was so alive, and I watched, mesmerized, as cars sped through the maze of roads and the city before us twinkled with vitality. It was like the city itself was a living, breathing thing, and it reminded me that no matter what, I would never truly be alone.

I was starting to see why a good view was important to her. She was alone more than anybody I had ever known. Maybe she really did like spending time with me.

"Do you like it?"

Her voice was so soft I almost didn't recognize it. I looked at North. She was entranced by the show before us, an expression on her face that was impossible for me to identify. It made me feel a little bit sad for her, whatever it was.

"Yes," I whispered. Her gaze remained on the scene for a moment, but her lips curled into a slight smile.

"I'm glad."

Finally, she inhaled and squared her shoulders with determination before meeting my eyes. "There's so much I want to show you."

I had no idea what to say to that. I wasn't even sure I could trust her, but the way she was acting was making me start to wonder if there was something wrong.

"Are you all right, North?"

She laughed, a pained expression sweeping over her face as she looked down to the floor. "Read a room, Finch. I'm not here to talk about my problems."

"I just…"

North shook her head and gripped me gently by the waist. "I said I don't want to talk about it."

She tugged me toward her, and suddenly her warm lips were against mine and I found myself lost in her taste. God, she felt good. I allowed myself to hold her as we kissed, losing myself in the peaceful perfection of the night. When she pulled away from me, her eyes were glassy, almost as if she were trying not to cry.

"I need to ask you something," she said, stilling her hands to linger on my waist.

"Ask me."

"Come to Europe with me," she said. "We just bought you a wardrobe to last two months, easily. We'll leave tomorrow. We can go back to Chicago; you can get your passport and your cat. And we can go to Europe. I'll show you everything you want to see, Aria. And we'll be safe there."

My arms slipped from her torso and fell to my sides. Go to Europe? *Tomorrow?*

"North," I said, shaking my head. "I can't."

Her face fell and she looked away from me, her expression half obscured by the shadow left by the dimness of the lights.

"Please, Aria."

"I really can't," I said. Letting myself relax on an impromptu date night was one thing. But being constantly with North at the same time as trying to investigate her? That would be impossible. I couldn't do it. Even though, for some reason, there was a significant part of me screaming to say yes.

"It's okay, Finch. I understand."

She turned back to look at me and I was taken aback by the haunted expression on her face. The spell had been broken and both of us were standing in an awkward silence, unsure of what to say next.

"Maybe…maybe it wouldn't be the worst thing, you know. To spend the night on a jet back to Chicago."

The words were like torture as I forced them out of my mouth, and North's haunted eyes now looked pained. "Right. Of course. Go ahead and gather your things, I'll have my driver escort you home."

I frowned. "You're not coming?"

"No. I'd like to be by myself tonight. Thank you, though, for coming with me. I had a good time."

I nodded, backing away from her to clumsily gather the numerous shopping bags that had accumulated on the floor.

"I should be thanking you. I had a great time. I'm sorry about…" I paused, having no clue how to apologize for something that felt like it was tearing my soul apart.

She nodded and walked away, typing briskly on her cell phone. A few moments later, there was a soft knock at the door.

"Good night, Finch," North said, hanging back in the darkness. She had turned back to look out the window so that I couldn't see her face.

"Good night."

I spent the next two hours alone on North's private jet, wondering why in the hell it hurt so much to tell her no.

CHAPTER THIRTY-FOUR

When I made it back to my apartment, even the sight of my happy little cat wasn't enough to cheer me up. All I wanted to do was to go back to the city and take back my words, figure out what in the hell had been bothering North so much. How could I have left her alone like that? The fierce desire to protect her was back, but protect her from what? I couldn't do any kind of protecting from Chicago when she was alone in New York. The memory of deserting her in that beautiful room that she'd planned to share with me made me feel like a monster.

I was scared for her, with a knot in the pit of my stomach the size of the portion of lasagna that she had put away that night, but I didn't know why. She'd said we would be safe in Europe, which implied that we weren't safe here in Chicago. Maybe not even in the country. Whoever had broken into the office to hurt her could have found her, done something more to her that she wouldn't tell me. Had something happened since the last time we'd seen each other? Why couldn't she ever seem to tell me the whole story?

Probably because she had too much to hide.

I wanted to call her. To try and heal the rift I'd created by blurting out the worst possible thing. I'd done it for a reason, though. I couldn't give so much of myself to her if she were the monster that everyone was saying she was. If I went along with her to Europe and gave my idiotic heart what it was screaming that it wanted, I could fall in love with someone I didn't really know.

If the way she was treating me was all an act, then I would be in even more danger than if I kept myself at a distance. Before I gave in to any more sex or any of her requests, I needed to be sure that she was someone worth falling for. Everything I had heard so far, even things out of her own mouth, told me otherwise. I couldn't make myself vulnerable to her again.

I sat down in the kitchen, my throat stinging with a stubborn lump that I couldn't swallow. Hot tears welled in the corners of my eyes, and I pulled the folder that Clayton had given to me toward me and began to half-heartedly look through it. I needed to remind myself that I had done the right thing. Otherwise, I would never be able to forgive myself for the way the night had ended.

Article after article painted North as a horrible human being. Photos of her in questionable situations, speaking to questionable people. Documents from Malaysia, maps of a slave trade route, photos of the hardened North with the cold, tired eyes that looked vaguely the way she had looked when she'd asked me to leave with her to go to Europe. I could see it all there, in black and white, but it still didn't make sense.

Because beyond those pictures, I saw the woman embracing her grandmother and smiling at my cat. I felt the gentleness behind her touch and the determination she had to make the world a better place. I was either very brainwashed or very loyal. Maybe just stupid.

When I looked more closely at the documents that were supposed to be from Acquati Technologies, I began to notice strange little details that didn't add up. The logo was off-center. North's signature didn't look right either. And there was the fact that several of the departments that were listed on the papers didn't even exist. At least, not to my knowledge, though they did seem familiar somehow. I'd been searching through Acquati's network for the past month and felt confident that I would know whether or not I was seeing authentic evidence of transactions made by the company itself. But the longer I looked, the less convinced I became.

What could it possibly mean? It certainly looked like someone was doing business with Malaysian slave traders for sweatshop labor, but was it really Acquati Technologies? More importantly, who would gain from posing as them to do their business? It didn't make sense. And if it wasn't AT, why were there so many pictures of North making these transactions? I couldn't say for sure without scanning them for analysis, but they didn't appear to be doctored in any way. Something was off, I just couldn't figure out what.

I sighed and stuffed the papers back into their folder. I was exhausted from the day. It had taken a hell of an emotional toll on me. Was jet lag really a thing? Or had I just allowed myself to once again be steamrolled by my feelings for North?

Just as I climbed into bed, I heard my phone ring. I answered quickly, hoping it was the devil herself. But, of course, it wasn't. I had rejected her with a harshness I hadn't even known I was capable of.

"Aria, hey!" Thom said cheerfully. I'd forgotten that he had planned to call. "I hope it's not too late for me to be calling."

I rolled onto my stomach and hid my head beneath my pillow. "No, it's all right. How's your work thing going?"

"It's great so far. When we get back, I'm so going to make you try Malaysian food. It's freaking fantastic. I never knew."

My stomach dropped. "What?"

"Oh, you don't like it?"

It felt as if my mouth had filled with cotton. "No, Thom. I don't like it."

"Bummer. I'm running out of good date ideas."

"Hey, I hope you don't mind, but I'm actually really tired. I was just getting into bed."

"Oh…I thought you said it was all right."

"It just hit me."

"No worries. Let's talk tomorrow, okay?"

"Sure," I said, trying to keep the strain out of my voice. "Good night."

"Night!"

We hung up, my blood curdling. Thom was in Malaysia. The same place where the cryptic email to North had come from. How could that be a coincidence? He'd been hanging around me since not long after I'd been hired into Acquati Technologies. He had access to my apartment and had probably gone through everything. He'd had free roam of my things, and I had been a total idiot to allow it. Thom, who spent his time snooping around my PC and making me bad lasagna, was in Malaysia. Thom, whose heart North had declared black.

I'd spent so much time demonizing North in my head that I hadn't given any of my suspicion of Thom any merit. Had I had the wrong person all along? He had to be involved, but how? Was he working for her? Against her? Spying on me? What the hell was going on?

I was wide awake after the phone call and sat up in bed, too rigid to sleep, and worked at the wooden box absently until light began streaming through my windows. It seemed like the more I learned, the more questions I had. And like the frustrating wooden puzzle, I would never get anywhere close enough to the truth. Not until it killed me.

CHAPTER THIRTY-FIVE

"North isn't here today," Sandra said curtly.

I frowned, puzzled. "But North is always here."

I'd been trying to get in touch with her all weekend, hoping that maybe some subtle questioning would help me get some answers about the information that I'd seen in the file Clayton had given me. Every time I tried calling her, it went straight to voice mail. I guess I'd had it coming for how often I had done the same to her.

"Well, not today," Sandra informed me, her tone doing nothing to conceal her annoyance. "In fact, she hasn't been in since Friday. She didn't even call me about it."

That was strange. Maybe North had decided to stay in New York over the weekend. Was it because of me? I hadn't expected her to take my rejection so hard.

"All right…thanks."

Sandra didn't even acknowledge me. I sighed and headed back to my office. If North knew who was trying to slander her, then maybe I would be able to figure out what was going on. Maybe she wasn't being slandered at all, but I hadn't been able to shake the feeling that the file had given me. Just as I'd suspected, when I checked the images thoroughly for signs of photo manipulation, they hadn't revealed any tampering.

My feelings had been stormy at best since I'd gotten home. I thought maybe I would feel better being able to talk to North, but she was better at avoiding me than I had ever been at avoiding her. Now, she was nowhere to be found, and it was most likely my own fault. I would just have to keep trying to put the pieces together myself.

When I made it back to my office, my cell phone rang. I didn't recognize the number, but I answered it anyway. If North was trying to contact me somehow, I didn't want to miss the chance to talk to her.

"Have you decided what you're going to do?"

I recognized Clayton's voice and sighed. How the hell was I supposed to decide what to do when nothing was clear? Not only did North look suspicious, but now Thom did too. Then again, Thom's picture wasn't in the Ivys' files.

"You do realize that you're calling me at work, right?" I said, plunking myself down into the plush chair North had chosen for me.

Clayton didn't acknowledge my words. "Acquati Technologies is going to make their move soon. If we don't expose them, it will be too late. Once the gears are put in motion, from there it will be impossible to connect our information to them."

"Why is that?" I asked, leaning back in my seat. My eyes scanned the office, then settled on the sun as it began to stream in through my window. Mornings here sure had the potential to be peaceful. You know. If anything in my life could be simple.

"Once the work has been sourced out to the laborers, there are networks out there that make it incredibly dangerous to try and expose them. These people have been doing what they do for a long time, and once there is profit in it for them, any threats to that profit are easily eliminated."

"So, you'd rather they eliminate me than you, right?" I scoffed.

"No, it's not that. You have an in at the company that we don't. Unless you're only reluctant because North's gotten in your head. We could use your help in getting this to the public before it's anyone's life at stake."

"How do you know that people's lives aren't already at stake?"

North's life.

"This is a serious matter, and we are doing what we can with what we have. Come on, Finch. I thought you were stronger than this. Have you gone soft? The damage Acquati does will only grow as time moves on, and we need to act fast. I need to know if you're going to help us or not."

I sighed. If I refused to help them, they might clam up and stop sharing information with me. If I agreed to help them, North might find out that I was working to shut her down before I was ever able to make progress. Regardless of any of it, I still didn't know the truth, and I didn't want to act until I did. I wouldn't feel right about persecuting North until I knew what it meant that Thom was in Malaysia and that her supposed files looked, in my opinion, forged. Even if the pictures weren't.

"I'm doing my best," I said, and hung up before Clayton could say anything more. I was feeling the pressure from all sides now, and it was starting to feel like too much. If I could just get the chance to talk to North about this again, maybe I would be able to figure out the right questions to ask.

I dialed her number again, but, as I expected, all I heard was the message on her voice mail.

"This is North, leave a message."

I opened my mouth, then thought better of it and hung up. There was too much to say, and no way to possibly say it. So, I did what came most naturally to me. I focused on what was left of my work.

CHAPTER THIRTY-SIX

The next few days were quiet at Acquati Technologies, and we all went on as usual. Soon, however, North's absence became impossible to ignore. There wasn't much more I could do with my designated work without her input, so on the third day of her cold shoulder, I went home early to focus on the puzzle she had left me. It was better than dwelling on all of the unanswered calls and emails that I had sent.

I had been making incremental progress in figuring out how to get into the box but still had a lot to figure out. I could tell I was close, though. I was sitting on the couch with Bilbo, watching the news and pressing a piece into place when North's picture suddenly appeared on the screen. I gasped and sat the box down, leaning forward in my seat. Bilbo jumped off the couch, distressed by my sudden movement.

"North Acquati, Founder, CEO, and Chair of Acquati Technologies, is missing."

My heart dropped to my stomach, and I grabbed the remote to turn the volume up, my hands trembling. All I could see in my mind was the expression in North's eyes when I'd left her alone at the hotel. It was as if she had somehow known that this was going to happen. And I'd abandoned her there. I swallowed hard, forcing myself to focus on the rest of the broadcast. I needed to know everything.

"Ms. Acquati was last seen boarding her private jet in New York City on Saturday morning. She hasn't been seen or heard from since. She was reported missing Tuesday afternoon by her bodyguards, who had been told to remain posted for Acquati's return. Investigations are ongoing. If you have any information on the whereabouts of North Acquati, contact your local authorities as soon as possible to ensure her safe return."

The broadcast changed to a story about how sugar causes wrinkles as if they hadn't just given me the most horrifying news of my life. I stood up, trying to fight the bile that was rising in the back of my throat. It felt like the world was crashing down around me.

I paced my apartment, trying to calm myself down enough to think. All I could do was imagine the worst. The bruises on North's body the night the company had been broken into. Her eyes begging me to escape with her to Europe, to keep us safe.

"Fuck!" I growled to nobody in particular. Bilbo watched me with wide eyes from his little cat tree. I pressed my fingers against the bridge of my nose and inhaled deeply. I had to calm down and think. She had last been seen getting on her private jet. The jet hadn't returned to Chicago. Had she gone into hiding in Europe? Or had her jet been hijacked by the same people who had broken into her office?

Damn it, North. Why hadn't she just been able to tell me what was going on? What good did it do either of us for me to be a sitting duck?

My phone rang suddenly, and I picked it up, answering vacantly as I tried to figure out what I was going to do.

"Aria, I just heard. Are you all right?"

"Thom? Yeah, I'm all right," I said, narrowing my eyes. I hadn't spoken with Thom since I'd realized that his work trip had taken him to Malaysia. If he was involved in any of this,

I had to stay in touch with him. I couldn't let on that I was suspicious, but I also needed to know more about where he was at. Malaysia was an entire country, and if North had disappeared and Thom was involved somehow, I needed to know where to go. Because as the seconds raced by, my mind knew there was only one thing for me to do.

I was going to get her back.

"I'm glad. I was worried that maybe the two of you had been together when she disappeared. I never know what's going on with you."

"Yeah, I'm sorry about that, Thom. Really…" I paused, overwhelmed suddenly by the reality that I had no idea how to feel toward him or anyone else at the moment. There were things I had felt, like guilt for the way I had put him in second place when it came to North, but now all I felt was confused.

I had a mission, though, and I had to stick with it.

"I wish I could just get out of here for a while," I admitted. At least that part wasn't a lie.

"If I were there, I would let you stay with me."

"What if I just bought a ticket and met you in…well, where are you?"

"You really want to just come to Malacca?" Thom said with a laugh. "I don't know if you'd like it here."

"Come on, I've never even been out of the country," I said, a spark of elation surging through me as another piece of North's puzzle clicked into place in my hands. I hadn't even registered my hands working at it absently. It had become almost a nervous habit to try and solve it.

"I mean, if that would make you feel better. I know I would feel better about it. Whatever is going on at Acquati, it can't be good. I could protect you here."

"Protect me? From what?"

Thom was quiet for a moment. "Well, I'm not sure, but your boss is missing. There are rumors of foul play. But you didn't hear it from me."

I frowned. "What kind of foul play?"

"Aria, North might not be who you think she is. It's better if you don't get too involved in any of it. Come stay with me. At least until everything blows over. Bring Bilbo. My company can get his quarantine waived."

Join Thom in one of the most bustling human trafficking hubs in the world? That sure sounded safe. Especially upon realizing that there was a very high chance that he was involved in whatever was going on with North. Still, if she had disappeared anywhere due to foul play, wouldn't it be there? That's where all the documents from the Poison Ivys pointed. If nothing else, maybe I would get a better picture of what was going on.

As sketchy as it sounded, I knew I had to do something, and this was as good a first step as any. What would I do with the box, though?

I glanced down at it and let out a soft exclamation of surprise. I wouldn't have to do anything with the box. It was open.

"All right, Thom. I'll do it."

"Really?" He sounded genuinely shocked, but soon I could hear his smile through the phone. "Great. Let me know the details of your flight and I'll pick you up. This is awesome!"

I swallowed hard, clenching the box tightly.

"Yeah. Awesome."

I chatted absently with him for a few more moments before I hung up. My heartbeat was ringing in my ears, and I lowered myself onto the couch, taking deep, slow breaths to try and calm myself. It was time to learn all of North's secrets.

CHAPTER THIRTY-SEVEN

Good job, Finch. You figured it out.

Just like I knew you would.

Unfortunately, this letter isn't going to give you all of the answers. If I could tell you everything outright, I would. I just can't let my troubles become your troubles. This means more to me than any of my other projects ever have, or I would have been more transparent about it. Unfortunately, its success depends on our discretion.

I think you'll get the idea soon enough, though. And when you do, you will know exactly what to do with the information that I have provided to you. I might not be around long enough to see this project through to its completion, but I hope you are. I need you to be.

Some of what you will find in this box are personal effects. Sentimental items I have accumulated over time. Things I don't trust in the hands of anybody else. If, or more likely, when, something happens to me, please see to it that they are returned to my family in Lecco, Italy. But don't jump the gun, Finch. Make sure you have everything you need before you do so.

Thank you for your loyalty and for being a faithful employee. I'm glad I got to meet you, and I appreciate all you've done for Acquati Technologies. And for me.

Yours,
North

I don't know how many times I read North's letter before gaining the confidence to look through the various other items in the box. She had packed them with typical North-like care, securing every little thing tightly in its own compartment, stored in sleek black boxes and fastened in with bubble wrap and Velcro. I would have laughed at the organizational perfection of it all if the situation didn't feel so bleak.

Why had she chosen me as the recipient on that fateful day that seemed so long ago? Back when I lived and breathed for the glimpses of North I would get from my cubicle, the days I would put a thousand percent into my work, hoping to get her attention or a nod or one of those heart-stopping smiles?

When had she decided I was the one who could help her with, well, whatever this was? Or had I made it obvious just how pathetically devoted to her I was? What was it she'd said on the phone to Donnie? "She's like putty in my hands"?

She wasn't wrong. Still, it hurt to hear her say it like that.

I inhaled deeply, pushing the thoughts away. I had to get through this before I went to Malaysia. I considered letting the authorities know what I knew, but to be honest, I had no idea what I really knew. Neither would the police. For all I knew, they might take me into custody for being one of the last people to know North's whereabouts. If I was locked up for questioning, what help would I ever be able to offer her? Sure, the police had more manpower, but would they be able to solve North's puzzles and get to her in time, before anything happened to her? I still wasn't quite there yet. She had told me as much in her letter.

I could hand the box and everything in it over to the police for them to analyze. Maybe it could help them to figure things out and get her home safely. It would be impossible for me to do it, though. She had been so adamant about keeping the police out of it last time that it almost didn't even seem like an option anymore.

Besides that, I had worked so hard to get to the heart of the puzzle. Handing it over now for someone else to figure out would kill me. She had trusted me with the information, whatever it was, for a reason. And if something happened to her and I turned her things in to the police and never got them back, how would I live with myself? What if I never got *her* back?

I began to look through the box's contents with clumsy hands, my heart drumming so powerfully in my chest that I could feel it in my ears. There were a few old pictures inside an envelope of North and her family, and letters that were written in Italian. I frowned, my paranoia mounting. If I was capable of breaching other people's Internet security in order to spy on people, it would be easy for them to do the same to me. If that meant they had spyware on my devices that was too sophisticated for me to catch, I'd have to be careful. I could use my phone for a translation, but that would mean they would know exactly what I was translating before I did. I refused to do anything that could further jeopardize North. I would need to do these translations the old-fashioned way: with a pen, paper, and patience.

I wouldn't have time to translate them before my flight, but maybe I would be able to make some progress during, if I could miraculously find an English-Italian dictionary. If I left early enough, I could pick one up on my way to the airport, assuming the cab driver wouldn't mind keeping an eye on Bilbo while I ran inside.

Did I want to leave my cat with a random cab driver? Hell, no. I would go out and buy dictionaries that night. One for Italian and one for Malaysian. Oh, god. What was I getting myself into?

I cast the letters aside (as painful as it was for me to do so) and began to examine the rest of the box's contents. There was an old compass. It looked like an antique. I assumed it must be one of the sentimental effects that North had mentioned in her letter. If she didn't come back from wherever she was, it would be going back to North's family in Italy.

I studied the craftsmanship and frowned when I realized that no matter where I moved, the compass stayed stubbornly pointed to the east. In fact, the needle was bouncing as if in a tight circle, looping around its axis to keep itself pointing east. It made me a little dizzy to focus on it, so I put it down with the other things and continued looking through the box.

My heart nearly stopped when I pulled out an obituary with North's face on it. It was written in Italian, but the name said "Levante Acquati." North's sister. The twin who had died. Of course.

My eyes scoured the dates, and sure enough, just as North had told me, her sister's death had taken place a year ago. She'd been killed, North had said. That was an unusual way to report a death in the family. Most of the time, unexpected deaths were because of accidents of some kind. What had happened to Levante? And why hadn't I ever thought to learn Italian?

There wasn't much else of note in the box. Still more documents in Italian, a ring that immediately made me think of North's nonna, and a copy of Acquati Technologies' mission statement. I must have read it a million times before. Why put that in there? It was on the website as public knowledge. I scanned the document and focused on the date. She had written it the week after her sister had passed away.

When I read the statement, my eyes widened. This was not what I had expected to find.

Acquati Technologies: Devoted to bringing down the bastards who killed my sister, no matter what the cost.

CHAPTER THIRTY-EIGHT

My stomach fluttered as I strapped into my seat on my first flight. I'd have plenty of time to research the letters between layovers and time in the air. It was almost a relief to have something to do to dwindle away the long hours. I needed a distraction from the thought of North somewhere out there in trouble…or worse.

I swallowed hard as the plane began to move forward on the runway, thinking of the comforting way that North had taken my hand during the takeoff and the landing of her private jet. What I wouldn't give for a chance to live that night over. My chest grew tight as I realized that I might never see her again.

No. Failure wasn't an option. I would do everything that I could. I would translate every single word in the Italian language if that's what it would take. I'd visited the bookstore the night before after securing North's belongings back exactly as she'd left them. I had them tucked into my awkward little purse right under the crook of my arm.

I had a window seat, and fortunately no other passengers had been seated beside me. Bilbo was my faithful traveling companion, snoozing in his carrier in front of me, blissfully unaware of his first ascent into controlled airspace. I sighed, wishing he could be curled up in my lap for his aeronautic nap, but unfortunately that wasn't the way of the world. We'd be together soon enough. I only hoped the same would be true of me and North.

I decided to keep my mind occupied by starting on the translations of the letters in North's box. It was a tedious undertaking, and I had to wait until we had made it into the air and were moving along at a steady pace, but eventually I managed to get started without suffering from motion sickness. North's little trick with the peppermints had lingered in my mind, so I'd taken some with me for the flight, just in case. It was a good thing I did.

I managed to get into a groove, translating the first of North's letters slowly but surely. It had been at the top of North's meticulous pile, and I had been careful not to disrupt her organizational system. It had to mean something. Everything she did seemed to be layered with meaning.

The letter was to North from her sister; I knew that before I even got near the end. I recognized her name from the obituary. Levante Acquati, with love.

It took me probably two hours before I had anything resembling a coherent letter. When I was finished, I closed the dictionary with a victorious little thump and reclined so that I could read it in comfort. My back and neck ached a little bit from staying hunched over the little tray where I'd been working, and it felt good to stretch out.

Beloved sister;

You will never believe what Pablo told me. I have had a great opportunity given to me! We will be leaving Lecco in three days' time. From there he has a great business opportunity. He tells me we will be millionaires! Of course, I could never compete with my darling sister. You know how I am. I enjoy boys and pretty things far more than the boring details of running a company. Maths and sciences are horribly dull, but I am so proud of you and your successes. You are quite a sister to have!

Can I tell you a secret? Some days, people will approach me and think that I am you. Do you mind terribly if I give them an autograph? I hope not, because I already have, though I fear my signature may not compare, despite how much practice I get.

Oh, North, I am so excited to leave Lecco! I thought about New York the other day. Mama and Papa seemed so happy there. I know it hurt them that I decided to stay behind here with Antonio. How silly I must have looked when things didn't work out with him. I am lucky for Nonna. Don't tell our parents, but she helped me to afford a place of my own after he left. They told me very firmly that they wouldn't help me anymore. And before you get angry for not coming to you first, please don't. I can't stand the way you scold me over my boyfriends. If I have to hear one more lecture about my stupidity, I wouldn't be able to bear it, especially from my oh-so-successful sister. I will make it on my own.

Especially with Pablo by my side. With him I feel anything is possible! You would like him a lot. Wait, what am I saying? You never like any of my lovers. Perhaps you need to know love yourself before you understand. When are you going to stop being such a hermit and allow yourself a companion? I swear it will change you for the better. Not that you could be much more perfect. Nonna keeps that magazine cover of you in a frame, did you notice?

I laughed out loud there. I had noticed.

Anyway, I hate to bore you more with details of my droll life. I just wanted to write and let you know that my address will be changing, so if you try to send me any packages or gifts (the last was so beautiful! I wear it every day), I will not receive them here. When I arrive and we are settled in, I will write you with our new address. For now, I must finish my packing. Please think about what I am saying—find a lover and enjoy it! There is nothing quite like it.

With all my love,
Levante

I set my translated version of the letter down and mulled it over. It appeared that North and her sister were polar opposites. What a personality she must have had. It was obvious that they had adored one another, despite the differences. It was no wonder that North wanted revenge.

There didn't seem to be anything very revealing in the letter, but I tucked the translation into the box and started on the next. It was going to be a long flight.

CHAPTER THIRTY-NINE

I proceeded with my hack translations of the next documents in the stack during the interminable flights and layovers over the next thirty-two hours. The first one was a personal ledger that North had kept, receipts to Italy for large sums of money. I had seen some documents similar to this one in Clayton's folder, which I'd left back at my apartment. If Thom was involved and his henchmen went through any of my belongings while I was in Malacca with him, I would have a hell of a time explaining myself. The compass and letters might be a little easier if he found them, but now that I had figured out North's puzzle, at least I could lock them away if I needed to. They would be safe there.

I couldn't say the same for myself. All I could do was hope that if Thom was involved, I would be able to keep him off the trail. I had to figure out what to do before being there with him ended up costing me everything.

Once I'd finished with the receipts, I found another letter from Levante.

My beloved sister,

I should have known it was too good to be true. The home Pablo took us to was as extravagant as I'd imagined. Truly beautiful, almost like home! It overlooked the water, and we could see the boats gliding up and down the waterway cutting through the city's streets at night. What a fanciful arrangement. There was so much water and it was very beautiful.

Then other men started to come to the house and look at me. I don't know what they were saying. The natives of Malacca speak a tongue I do not understand. The men would look at me and point and gesture, arguing amongst themselves as if my being there was a great burden.

The strangest part was the quiet American man, whose blue eyes watched with steel while the others argued. He said nothing as their words escalated in volume, until finally he held up his hand and shook his head at Pablo. "Not here. It is too dangerous."

Eventually, Pablo grabbed me by the wrist so hard it left a mark and dragged me away. We had nowhere to go, and he demanded I contact you. I don't know what would have happened to me if you didn't respond, if you weren't able to give us the cash for a nice place to live. It is more peaceful without the strange men visiting, but I am afraid that they will be back.

Pablo will not tell me anything else about what is going on. Only that his plans for us to be rich are not what he thought. I think he is ashamed, and he drinks all day now and has such a ferocious temper. He is nothing like he was before we left. I regret coming here!

Thank you again for your help. I'm afraid I must ask you once again, though. I cannot afford another call right now. We are running out of food, and I would like to get a ticket back to Lecco. I hate to ask, but I know our parents would only be furious at me if I told them what has happened. They didn't want me to leave with Pablo and I don't want to give them the satisfaction of knowing they were right, or Nonna to have any reason to worry. Would you mind helping me again? This will be the last time I ask, I promise you. And not the kind of promise I used to make when I promised I wasn't responsible for taking your half of the biscotti. This is the kind of promise I make where I truly hope to be able to keep it and swear it is true.

I love you, my sister.
Levante

There were several other shorter letters from Levante that came after that, each of them more and more brief, asking North for money. A lot of the woman's spark seemed to fade over time, until I came to the last letter in the stack.

How could you deny your own flesh and blood? The person who shared a womb with you? What would your precious worshippers think of you if they knew what a selfish shrew you are? What if I came out with the story to the press about the time when we were nine years old and you nearly set fire to our home because you couldn't stand the sight of anything less than an average grade on your schoolwork, so you decided to burn it right in the bedroom? We could have all died because of your tunnel vision. Anyone who thinks you are the next coming is as blind as you are to the realities of the world. Don't bother talking to me again. I want nothing to do with you.

There were no more letters after that, and my chest tightened at the thought of this being the last correspondence that North had with her sister before she was killed. After the letter was a newspaper clipping in Malay with a picture of the water cutting through the city featured. I was glad I had decided to grab the Malay-English dictionary, but a little overwhelmed by the task. This was a much different type of language; translating it was going to be much more difficult.

I didn't get any rest on that flight. I worked, in a manic state, to translate whatever I could of the article before we landed. By the time the pilot's voice was over the loudspeakers, informing us to buckle our seat belts and prepare for landing, I had pieced together just enough of the article to understand the basic premise of what it was saying.

Levante Acquati had been found dead, her body floating in the Malacca River. They had ruled the death a suicide, but North had been convinced that it was murder. According to reports, her body was being shipped back to Italy to be buried in the family plot, and there was no foul play suspected.

Behind the newspaper article was a small envelope containing plane tickets to Italy, and then the obituary that was in Italian. I felt I had a pretty good grasp on what that would say after my painstaking effort to translate the newspaper article and hurried to put everything back in the box as I had found it before landing. Thom would be waiting for me at the airport, and I couldn't let him see any of it.

Soon, the plane was shaking with turbulence, and we bounced gently as the wheels struck runway. I wasn't ready to see Thom, but I needed to find North. When we landed, I went through security as quickly as possible, eager to have Bilbo with me before finding Thom. Once I was hugging the little carrier to my chest, I made my way out with my luggage and spotted Thom immediately. He was beaming at me as if he wasn't connected to the disappearance of the person I cared most for in the world, so I did everything I could to summon my own smile, letting it fade the second his arms wrapped around me in a hug that I couldn't get out of fast enough.

"Are you ready to go?" Thom asked.

"As ready as I'll ever be," I replied.

He took my luggage and offered to grab the cat carrier, but I tugged it away from him gently. He wasn't going to come near my cat any more then could be helped. He gave me a lopsided smile and shrugged, then led me out to his car. I ducked inside, and we drove along the road, my eyes fixed on the great river cutting the city in half, imagining the mirror image of North floating in the water. This had to be stopped. Whether it killed me or not, I would play the part that North had asked me to.

CHAPTER FORTY

"Welcome to my lovely abode!" Thom said, sweeping his arm out to present an apartment that was even messier than mine. At least I almost had a system. If I had the space, it would be more organized. Unfortunately, not everybody can afford a giant North-sized condo, so all of my belongings were cramped and smushed together. I didn't leave literal garbage anywhere. I just had too many things and not enough space for them all. And once in a while I got lazy with the laundry, but never for more than an evening.

Thom, however, had takeout containers that probably dated back to the prehistoric era. I tried not to let my distaste show on my face and clenched the cat carrier close to my chest. Would Bilbo even be safe here?

"Thank you," I managed, after a moment of absorbing the sobering reality that I had decided for myself. "It's nice."

"There's just the one bedroom," Thom said immediately, moving quickly to help me take off my coat. "I hope you don't mind. I mean I figure since we're...well. It shouldn't be an issue, right?"

I pursed my lips and shook my head quickly. "Nope," I said, my voice an octave higher than usual. "Not an issue."

I took a glance at the sofa and grimaced. No, I wouldn't be sleeping on the couch. It was filthy and filled with crumbs. But I knew a chubby little cat who wouldn't mind that. I stifled a laugh as a thought occurred to me. With living conditions like this, it wouldn't matter if Thom forgot to feed him or not. He would easily be able to fend for himself.

We stood in awkward silence for a moment before Thom let out a quick laugh. "I cleaned up for you."

I chuckled, then clamped my mouth shut as Thom's face fell. "Oh," I said, my cheeks reddening. "You were serious."

"I didn't think you'd mind a little bit of clutter," Thom said with a shrug. "Normally it's not this bad, but I've been really busy with work things."

Work things. Right.

A sudden, intrusive memory of North hovering over me in her office popped into my head, and I looked away from Thom before he could see the fire on my cheeks. He seemed alarmed by my sudden reaction.

"What's wrong, Aria?"

"Work things," I mumbled.

Where the hell was North? I had come all the way to Malaysia. I had to find her. Where would I even begin? I had to make a checklist or something. I couldn't risk Thom finding something like that, though, so I would have to try and trust my own scatterbrained mind. Translate the letters in North's box. Search Thom's apartment. Follow him to figure out more about his "work things." Maybe tap his phone. I would have to be quick about everything, and I would have to be efficient. As soon as I had some time to myself, I would be in for a lot of work. It had to be done, though. North needed to be found.

"Does that mean that you won't be around much?" I asked, trying my best to sound convincingly bummed out about it. To be truthful, it couldn't have worked out better for me if that were the case. I would have some time to myself to try and figure out what the hell was going on with North and how Thom was involved. Maybe he would even be able to lead me to her.

"I'm a busy man, Aria," Thom said, grinning. "But I will do my best to meet your demands."

I shuddered inwardly. If Thom was involved in this, the only demand I had for him was to rot in hell. Still, I could hardly say that to him, especially if I wanted to use him as a base of operations while I investigated him. Finding out if there was a connection between Thom and North might be my only chance to figure out where she was and find a way to help her if she needed it. So, I would play along.

I gave Thom a tight-lipped smile and a small nod. "Good, Thom."

"It's really good to have you here. I didn't think you'd actually come. Honestly, after everything, I expected you to get cold feet at the airport or something. It was kind of a shock to actually see you getting off the plane. I didn't think…" He hesitated, then offered me a quick twitch of a smile.

I frowned. "You didn't think what?"

"It just doesn't seem like you're that into me, sometimes."

Why a pang of guilt suddenly pounded in my chest I don't know, but it did. "It's not like that, Thom. You know how it is. Work things…"

Thom nodded slowly before his face brightened back into his bubbly demeanor. "Well, you won't have to deal with any of that here. You'll be safe, and neither of us will have to worry about Acquati Technologies interfering with your life."

If he only knew.

Still, I tried to match his upbeat attitude with one of my own, and although it was a valiant effort on my part, it did nothing to ease the awkward tension between us. I couldn't fake being into him. It wasn't in my programming. No matter how kind he had been to me, there was no way to shake my suspicion of him now, and it was impossible for me to want to be close. Especially now that it was clear to me what I wanted. I wanted North. But she was gone.

The awkward tension between us lasted the rest of the evening, until I pleaded to skip movie night so I could go lie down. Thom wasn't ready to sleep yet, which was a mercy, so I brought Bilbo and my purse in with me. I tucked the purse under my pillow, wanting to keep North's treasures safe. My chest was burning with pain and anxiety, and as if a tiny, furry psychic, Bilbo stretched out over it and soothed me to the best of his ability with a low, rumbling purr. I stroked his fur gently as tiredness brought a heaviness to my eyelids, vowing to myself to use this time in Malaysia to find North, no matter what the cost.

CHAPTER FORTY-ONE

It was blissfully quiet once Thom went to work, whatever that entailed. I considered questioning him about the specifics of his job, like any normal girlfriend might do at some point in the relationship, but I didn't want to make him suspicious. And the dodgier he got about certain topics, the more difficult it would be for me to restrain myself from blunt accusations. I didn't exactly have the best track record when it came to keeping my mouth shut. It was better to avoid the landmines all together.

I would figure out everything that I needed on my own. It had always been that way. I couldn't take any chances, especially with North's safety on the line. And, most likely, my own.

The first thing I did when Thom left, after picking at the lackluster breakfast he had made for us, was search the apartment. It seemed, however, that whatever "cleaning up" he'd done was to remove any evidence of his comings and goings. It was odd how I couldn't find a single trace of his name on anything. There were no papers, no letters, no receipts. It was a dead end. He didn't even have a computer, at least not one he left at the apartment. It was bizarre. I would have gone crazy if I didn't have my laptop. Wasn't he supposed to be some kind of IT guy? He could be an assassin for all I knew.

I also realized that when he had called me and I'd invited myself to Malaysia, the phone number was completely different from the one he'd used in the States, but that wasn't a huge surprise. A lot of people changed cell phone services when they went overseas. I tried to trace the number, but again, it didn't turn up any leads. If I could get my hands on his cell phone, maybe I would have a chance, but I wasn't going to count on it. I hadn't even seen it since I'd arrived. He was keeping it close. *Work things.*

I was frustrated by the lack of progress and decided to bring out North's box again. I turned it around in my hands, relishing in the masterful woodwork that had gone into creating such an elegant puzzle. Had she had it made? Or had she made it herself, somehow? I had a feeling that if she wanted it to contain her most important secrets, she wouldn't have trusted anybody else with its construction. I was a little blown away by the thought of her lithe fingers working tirelessly to craft something so beautiful, but it didn't surprise me at all.

"*You have to earn it*," she'd told me when I'd asked how to get the key. She hadn't been kidding about that. Maybe I hadn't been patient enough to get the key to the metal case from her, but I'd earned the secrets within.

I carefully opened the box again and took out the papers, just as she'd left them. Since searching Thom's place had been a bust, I would just keep trying to unravel North's mysteries. I was feeling a little burnt out with the translating, so I stalled by picking up the compass. My eyes followed the needle as it hovered in the east, doing its strange circular loop around it. It stayed fixed there, despite being on the literal other side of the world. Why would North keep a broken compass? Was it sentimental? She seemed like the kind of person who would have gotten it fixed, even if it *was* sentimental. Who could say, though? There was just too much that I didn't know.

I sighed and decided to put the compass away and get back to the letters. My heart gave a little tremor when I found one from North to her sister. It was impossible to say whether or not she ever actually sent it, as there was no envelope. It was in Italian like so many of the others, so I sighed and set to work in translating it.

My sister,

You know that I love you more than anyone! It hurts me so much that you think I am so cold. It also hurts me that you are taking advantage of me—I know you are, and it is probably all the idea of your partner in bed. How could you choose a man over your own mirror image? We shared a womb, but that does not mean I have to share my bank account just to keep your worthless man happy. He should be providing for you, protecting you. But the way you have been acting is selfish and unjust. How dare you make such accusations, all because he does not know when enough is enough and he wants to take all that I can spare!

I will not allow it, Levante. If you choose to stay with this man, I cannot give you another cent. It is clear it is not for you. It is for him. Is he an addict or something? Or is it much worse than that? I am willing to help you, but this man can go fuck himself. Get rid of him and you will have whatever I can spare. Stay, and suffer the consequences of your actions. Nonna and Papa may have spoiled you rotten, but that doesn't mean the rest of us have to do the same. Don't push me into Mother's camp, Levante. I'm warning you.

Give me a call when you get this letter. My number has never changed. It is only you who seems to lose it.

North

773-555-0146

I managed to get the letter translated, but in doing so, I also discovered something. I had absentmindedly looked up the translation for North's sister's name in the Italian-English dictionary, not realizing in the moment that it was a name rather than another Italian word that I didn't know. When I translated it, I realized that her name meant East.

I gasped and scurried to pull the compass back out. That couldn't be a coincidence. The needle hovering over the E. It wasn't magnetic. It almost looked electronic. Something that could be programmed. Computer things? Was the compass a clue rather than a sentiment? There had to be something more to it than that.

I examined every little piece of the compass's smooth, cool surface. My eyes widened when I saw a tiny screw, and I thanked everything that was holy that it was just the right size for the screwdriver that I'd brought with me in case of a glasses-mending fiasco.

With trembling hands, I removed the backing from the compass and let out a soft sigh of elation as a small, crumpled piece of yellow paper rolled out into my hand. It was an address that North had scrawled hastily onto a sticky note. To where, I had no idea, but I was going to find out.

But that wasn't all. Immediately, my computer geeky mind processed that there was no magnet in this compass at all. Rather, it was a small loop transmitter that was like a tiny cherry on a piece of cake I hadn't even known I was hungry for. It was responsible for the frequency that was causing the compass needle to steadfastly point east. I squinted at the tiny masterpiece for a moment, wondering how in the world North had managed to put it together so seamlessly. It was exquisite.

Well, the device itself was simple enough to put together, and didn't require an external power source, which meant it would likely run indefinitely (or at least until my slow ass managed to put the pieces to her puzzle together), but still. She was so *thorough*. There was no way of knowing I'd translate her sister's name into a letter on this compass. If I hadn't, she'd given me another clue. I'd have realized that there was electricity in there eventually, so I'd think to look *in* the compass rather than dismiss it as sentimental. That's why she'd cautioned me to make sure I had everything I needed before returning anything to her family.

Beneath the loop transmitter, there was the most beautiful little memory card I had ever seen, nestled right in as if it had been waiting for me all this time. Everything that North had been hiding was now in my grasp. All I needed to do now was look.

CHAPTER FORTY-TWO

I didn't have any time to look at the precious little memory card before I heard Thom's keys jangling at the door. I cursed under my breath and hurried to put everything away, trying not to lose track of the order of the papers in case it might make a difference.

"Aria, I brought you dinner," Thom called.

I finished hiding everything away just as the door opened and shut. I let out a relieved breath before poking my head out of the bedroom to greet him. "Oh, hey, thank you."

I meant it. I was hungry after everything that had happened, and Thom's cooking was truly the worst. The takeout smelled incredible, though, and my stomach rumbled helplessly. Bilbo perked up, too, and I shook my head at him.

"You've had enough crumbs, you lucky rascal," I scolded.

My heart broke as his eyes turned to saucers, so I ended up giving him his dinner a little earlier than usual before joining Thom at the table.

The food was good, and I was so elated about the memory card that it wasn't difficult to feign a good mood with Thom. We had a few laughs—he'd always had such an easy laugh—before finally turning in.

My good mood evaporated when Thom lay down beside me. I felt his hand on my hip and I winced, flinching away from him without even meaning to. His hand retreated backward and rested on his own side of the bed.

"Sorry. I just thought, maybe…"

"I'm still pretty jet-lagged." The lie came a little too quickly, but Thom nodded.

"That's okay. No problem. Rest well."

He leaned over to drop a stubbly kiss on my forehead, and I inhaled privately, trying to hide my agitation. This was all wrong. I didn't want to be with him, and now it was so much easier for me to admit that I truly never had.

Truth be told, it was nearly impossible for me to relax now that I had finally gotten another piece of the puzzle. Could the address be North's? Maybe she had gone into hiding or something. It was local. I could visit it the next time Thom was working. Maybe everything was finally clicking into place. I might see North again. Maybe she really was going to be okay.

* * *

I could hardly contain my excitement when Thom left. I dove right for the box and unlocked it to retrieve the crumpled-up sticky note that I'd found in North's compass. I had to go there. Maybe I would get to see her again. I could apologize about everything…and there was even a chance that she might forgive me.

I squinted at the address before managing to locate it on a map. With the help of my trusty dictionary and a bit of money that Thom had gifted me the day I'd arrived so I wouldn't have to bother with an exchange rate (I'd forced the equivalent of USD into his hand despite his protests), I was soon in a cab on my way to the mysterious address.

It took longer than I had anticipated. I was in the car for probably an hour and a half before we finally came to a stop. I handed the money off, knowing in my gut that I was being ripped off by the driver but too excited about the next step forward to care. I even tipped him.

My heart fluttered in my chest as the idea of seeing North again brought me to cloud nine. Then again, it was possible she wouldn't be there at all. Maybe it was something else. I just had a good feeling about it and had acted on impulse. As usual. Hopefully it wouldn't cost me my life. There was no going back now. I had to know.

I was standing in front of a stilted house with a roof that looked as though it were made of straw. It didn't really strike me as North's aesthetic, but I figured it was all the better if she were to be in hiding. It took me a few seconds of hyperventilating before I worked up the nerve to approach the door. I knocked with a trembling hand and clutched my purse in a tight fist, jerking it farther up my shoulder in a graceless move spurned on by anxiety.

It seemed to take a century before finally, the door creaked open and I caught sight of a pair of cautious, beautiful brown eyes.

"North!"

I rushed through the door before the poor woman even had the chance to open it fully. I kicked it closed behind me, afraid someone might see her, and embraced her tightly, my elation in full swing.

She grew rigid against my touch and I could feel her resisting. I knew we had parted on bad terms before, but I couldn't help myself. I was just so glad to see that she was alive.

"North! Oh my god. I'm so glad it's you!"

I squeezed her tightly against my body, a little bit discouraged by the fact that she hadn't returned the affection. I was sure she was still upset with me, though, so I just held on.

"I never meant for things to get so messed up. There was so much going on in my head. God, I should never have left you like that, I'm so sorry!"

I buried my head into her neck and dropped a soft kiss onto it, tears of relief beginning to prickle in my eyes.

She let out a yelp and jerked her head away from me. I heard the slap before I felt the tingling hot pain in my cheek. "*No!*"

I was stunned for a moment before I managed to stumble through an apology. "Shit. I'm sorry, I always choose the worst times to be forward like that. I shouldn't have..."

She wriggled herself free and fixed a look of utter horror upon me.

"*Perché mi stai toccando in questo modo? Non mi piacciono le donne!*"

I frowned, unable to comprehend the spoken Italian as I studied the woman before me. She crossed her arms over her chest and raised a brow expectantly, as if expecting an explanation.

"North, I'm sorry about everything, but please don't shut me out, you know I don't speak Ital—"

She shook her head again. "No! No, no, no. Not North." She pointed to herself enthusiastically. "*Levante.*"

CHAPTER FORTY-THREE

"Lev—"

My stomach dropped and a sudden heaviness turned my limbs to lead. I felt like I was going to pass out. "I need to sit down."

"*Dai!*" Levante threw her arms up in the air and looked up at the ceiling as if pleading with the gods. "Ach, come and sit, then," she said, her accent heavy and tone annoyed. "But only because you know my sister."

Levante dragged me by the arm toward a small love seat. I sat down and put my face in my hands.

"You're supposed to be dead," I managed to whisper.

"Well, I live. Why are you here? How did you find me?" she demanded.

I managed to look up at her through my fingers, and she let out a short, terse laugh that was nothing like North's. "You look like a scared child. Your face is so pale!"

"Some water would be nice," I mumbled.

"You get nothing until you explain yourself."

I let out a defeated sigh and offered out the crumpled little sticky note. I could barely keep hold of it with my trembling fingers. Levante snatched it away, then her face fell.

"She told you she'd be here?"

I shook my head. "Not exactly," I mumbled. "I think she led me to you. Or. I don't know. She wanted me to keep the address safe, maybe."

"Ah, now things are making sense," Levante said with a firm nod. She sat down across from me in a little wooden armchair and lounged to the side, letting her legs dangle off the arm in a relaxed manner. "You're the pretty nerd."

"And you're the dead twin."

"Ach. I was never really dead."

"So why did she tell me that you're dead?"

"Why did she tell me you are pretty?" I stared at Levante until her face cracked into an impish smile. "I kid, pretty nerd. She thought I was dead."

My blood ran cold, and I looked up sharply at Levante. I had read the letters. They were awful and hurtful. North must have been crushed to receive them. And then to find out her sister had died? Even though she hadn't? It was too much. I could see why North's mother wouldn't be Levante's biggest fan. "Were you really that desperate for a reaction from her that you would fake your own death?"

Levante was standing now, fast as lighting, her dark eyes glaring down at me. I flinched against the back of the couch, startled by her intensity.

"Do you want me to kick you out of my house? What business is my family to you, anyway?" Her voice was rising with every word she spoke. "Just because you go kissing on my sister doesn't mean you know anything about her!"

I let out a rueful chuckle. I had already learned that lesson by now. "You're right about that. But please don't kick me out. Not until I understand."

Levante sighed and dropped back down into the chair across from me, keeping her eyes fixed on me like a wild animal that could strike at any second. It was so bizarre to be staring at someone who looked so much like North, but who had none of her feeling. Not to say that Levante lacked passion. It was just that they were such different people. Why wouldn't they be? They were twins, not clones.

"She told only Donnie of my address. My parents are angry with me. They may think like you, that I faked my dying to hurt them. But I didn't. I didn't fake anything. I can't explain to them. It is too dangerous."

"Then what happened?" I asked, calming my tone. We wouldn't get anywhere by going into feral mode and ripping out each other's throats.

She hesitated. "I'm not supposed to say anything to anyone. If they found out where I am…"

"Who?"

Levante avoided my question. "Tell me your name."

I exhaled deeply. "My name is Aria," I said. "A lot of people just call me Finch."

Levante crinkled her nose. "Like the bird?"

"I guess so."

"I am not fond of birds."

"Come on. Enough. I came all the way from America to find your sister. I found you instead. You know she's disappeared, don't you? Please, help me understand what's going on here." Levante's eyes filled with tears almost instantly, and I grimaced. "I'm sorry, I know it's a sensitive subject."

"You know nothing," she snapped. "You know what this place is, yes?"

My mouth was so dry I could hardly speak, but I nodded. "I know that North was being accused of procuring slave labor here."

Levante let out a scornful laugh.

"It was all a ploy. The 'evidence' they have for this? It was all photos of me. My lover at the time, the man who brought me here, he did so to sell me to *them*. Because of my sister. Because she is special. And wealthy. Because we are twins, and I make a good…what do you call it? Stool pigeon."

"Stool pigeon?"

"I am not fond of birds," she said again.

"I don't understand," I said, closing my eyes in an attempt to sort out the information that was now floating in my brain. "North is being set up by people who kidnapped you and forced you to pose as her."

"Yes."

"They wanted to make it look like Acquati Technologies was guilty of using slave labor?"

"Yes. Nobody wants North to succeed in a world like this. Don't be stupid, Aria."

"I just can't believe it…" She had worked so hard her entire life, and what had she gotten for it? Well, famous, for one thing. But look what it had done to her family, and what it might have done to her.

"For their plan to work, the world had to think I was dead. Then there would be no other explanation for the awful pictures and documents. They've made me sign things. I have never been able to copy her signature. But they made me try. They've made so many threats and showed me photos of what happens to her when I don't comply. So, I complied. That's my *sister*. I couldn't stand the thought of her being hurt. I love her more than anyone."

I froze, the memory of North's voice saying the exact same thing on the phone with her brother. She had been talking about Levante. All this time. I sighed, pain spiraling through my chest at the memory of North's bruised body. Levante loved her more than anyone. So did I.

"Do you know where she is now?" I asked.

Levante's eyes filled once again with tears. "No."

"How did she find out you were alive?" I asked.

Levante smiled. "My sister is a brilliant woman. It didn't take very long. There are people who want to see her company fail, and people who seek justice. One of the justice seekers sent a photo to North. I was in a bank. She saw it and knew straight away that I was in trouble."

"She came to save you," I murmured. "Just recently?"

"It has been a few months, but yes, it was somewhat recent. She found me somehow, money can help you do crazy things. She tried to get the Italian and American Embassy involved, but they move at a snail's pace. So, she came for me herself with hired guns. Men who were willing to die for North. She used their loyalty to save me."

Levante stared toward the window and shook her head, her expression forlorn. "Two men have died for me, Aria. I don't know how to live with it."

"Don't think about it that way," I said, my tone quiet. "They were loyal to your sister and her cause. She wanted to save you."

Levante's eyes sparkled as she fixed her dark gaze on me again. "North wanted to do so much more than that."

The way Levante used North's name in past tense made my stomach knot.

"And she will," I vowed, standing up and looking Levante in the eye. "I'm going to help her. Do you have any idea where she might be?"

Levante shook her head.

"After North liberated me, they want revenge. She set me up here and told me that if they were going to take one of us, that it was her turn to suffer. She wanted to do the legal thing, go through the embassy, get me to America. Danger, though, it is building, and she has changed the plan. I am supposed to wait here for a jet directly to America. I guess that was why she gave you my address. If they took her then she could be anywhere. They move around so often. I was never in the same place twice. They kept me blindfolded, it was very disorienting."

"I'm so sorry that happened to you," I said. I couldn't imagine it. No wonder North had been so despondent and hardworking. She didn't just want to succeed. She was fighting a war that none of us knew anything about. If she had said anything, they surely would have killed her sister. For real, this time. She had done her best to play the long game. The smart game. I wasn't going to let her down. "I'm going to find her. Nothing will keep me from making sure she's safe."

"She told me she had a pretty nerd who would make sure her plan was a success." Levante smiled sadly. "She wasn't wrong. But if you kiss me again, I will punch your pretty mouth."

I laughed at the unexpected brutality. "Fair enough," I said. "Listen, I don't know if you have access to a phone or not, but take my number. Call me if you think of anything else. Don't leave a message—only speak if it's me directly. And I will come back here the second I know anything about North, okay?"

"Okay," she said, her voice small. "Thank you, Finch-bird."

I smiled. "Don't thank me until North is safe."

Levante nodded, and I let out a heavy sigh. It hadn't been the breakthrough I had been hoping for, but I was almost there. Nothing would stop me now.

CHAPTER FORTY-FOUR

"Aria, what are you doing?"

I froze, my heart suddenly roaring in my ears. I had been tearing Thom's apartment apart, looking for clues to North's whereabouts in the brief time I had left after visiting Levante. He'd come in too soon for me to clean up evidence of my exploration, and the smell of takeout filled the small space with him.

"I was looking for a blank notebook. I'm so bored," I said, hiding my face before Thom could note any insincerity in it.

To my relief, he let loose an easy chuckle and reached around me to pluck a notebook from the shelf. He plopped it on the coffee table beside the bag of takeout. "What do you want a notebook for?" he asked, rather than interrogating me further for the mess I had made of his already catastrophic bookshelves.

"I was thinking about doing some doodles or something. I didn't realize how boring it would get to be off work for so long." I paused, wanting to be as believable as possible. "I can't connect to the Internet here. My phone service doesn't work, and when I tried using your phone to fix it, they started giving me shit for not informing them about my trip and verifying my identity before leaving. I have to wait two days before I can even use my credit card. Not only that, but with you gone, it's like the time slows to a crawl. There's nothing to do."

"Well, I think it's a good thing that you've been off work. You've needed a break for a long time, Aria. That woman ran you ragged." I pursed my lips. That was one way to put it. "I was afraid I'd see you have a breakdown or something. You're always so tense."

"My natural state, I'm afraid."

I cringed, my own words reminding me of the woman I was searching for more than myself. When in my life had I ever said "I'm afraid" before? Maybe I had and just didn't realize it. North was on my mind so much now that everything I did could remind me of her in one way or another. There was a growing presentiment in my chest as every second ticked by without knowing where she was or what was happening to her. As soon as Levante had revealed the realities of North's situation to me and things had started clicking into place, I felt more in over my head than ever.

"Well, I hope that some good comes of your doodles," Thom said. "If you need a pen, I think I had some on the desk over there." He nodded to a corner where, to be truthful, I hadn't even noticed a desk sitting.

"Desk, got it. Thank you."

Thom smiled and kissed me on the forehead. "I've got to head out, but I will be home in a few hours."

"Sounds good," I lied. I was already dreading it, and he hadn't even left yet.

He gave me a bright smile before disappearing outside, and as soon as I was sure he'd gone, I resumed my snooping. I was at the end of my rope in a search that got me nowhere, and I decided to brave the heap of clothes that Thom had called a desk. I was about to give up entirely when I tugged at a stubborn drawer. I thought it was locked, but upon a third, frustrated tug, it flew open at me and I gasped.

There was a gun lying over a full-sized picture of North. I was beside myself with panic and looked around the room as if the dirty clothes and piles of takeout containers would somehow guide me. I closed my eyes and took a deep breath before deciding to grab an old shirt and lift the gun from the drawer. I didn't want to leave any trace of myself on these things, but I had to know.

With my other hand tucked inside my shirtsleeve, I pinched the picture of North and held it up, examining it closely, my heart thudding dully in my ears. Her bright brown eyes would normally be smiling at me, but they looked tired and worn. I squinted, bile rising in my throat as I studied her surroundings. She was in a large room, sitting on the floor in the corner, her brow curled in a defiant, resentful expression. It looked like the walls were made of cement, and her hands were bound with a thick rope. There was a tray of what could almost be considered food beside her. Still, she didn't look defeated in the least.

My hands were shaking furiously as I turned the picture over, hoping for any other clue as to where she might be. I was shocked when, as simple as if the universe had told me it was time to stop searching, I found an address scrawled in pencil on the back of the photo. What the hell had Thom done to her?

I let out a growl of rage and stuffed the photo in my pocket and grabbed my jacket. I couldn't stay here, not with him. Not like this. I packed as quickly as I could and, with shaking hands, took Bilbo in his carrier along with my things to get a cab. It took all I had to keep my composure long enough to find us a hotel, but eventually I managed to. I released my cat, who was wide-eyed and agitated by all the change, and then, making sure I had everything I needed, I left the hotel. I was going to help her, even if it killed me.

CHAPTER FORTY-FIVE

I had never felt more anxious in my life than when I headed to the address on the back of North's photo. I didn't know whether or not I should involve the authorities. I wanted to, but how would I know if they would really be on my side? There was no way of telling what might happen, and I couldn't bear the thought of them telling me to stand aside while they dealt with it. Every second she was in there, my world lost a little bit more air.

I had to see her. It was reckless. It was stupid. I knew all of that. Still, if North had taught me anything, it was to be proactive. That was exactly what I intended to do.

I knew I should be smarter about it all. It wasn't going to end well for me. Unlike North, I was disposable. I wasn't the face of some huge multi-million-dollar corporation. I wasn't an identical twin who could play the patsy in their little scheme. And I certainly wasn't going to be good for much as far as their plans went unless they could somehow tell by my face that I was good with computers. They could kill me on sight, and they wouldn't think twice. Whoever "they" happened to be.

As the thoughts raced through my head, none of them seemed to matter. What mattered to me was that I knew where North was and that I had to see her and fix things somehow. No matter what that might mean for us. Or for me. Maybe I would live to regret it. Maybe I wouldn't live at all. I wasn't thinking clearly enough to run to some foreign police officials and implore them for help. I couldn't even speak the right language, and without my phone and the will to find one before going after North, all I had to rely on was myself.

I had a taxi take me to the neighborhood where the address was located. It was chilly that day, or maybe I just couldn't stop shaking from the adrenaline that had taken over my body. I made my way to the exact address on foot, not wanting anyone to be alerted to my presence. When I arrived, I saw a derelict old building made of red brick, lined with windows. Many of them were broken, and I shuddered, peering at them in the hopes of seeing inside. I couldn't, though, and as I listened, I didn't hear anybody around me.

I wasn't stupid enough to march through the front door, and instead opted to crawl around the perimeter of the building, looking through whatever windows I could see and trying to keep my wits about me. I drew the gun nervously before finally realizing the windows were painted from the inside and I wouldn't be able to look through any of them unless they were broken. With a little bit more patient investigation, I found one that was broken enough that I could fit through, so I removed my jacket and used it to clear out the broken glass and lower myself inside.

It took a few moments for my eyes to adjust to the darkness, and I squinted to try to gauge my surroundings. There were some big wooden crates shoved against the wall, and shelves. I was in a utility room of some kind. The walls were similar to the ones in the picture. North was close. I could sense it.

I crept carefully from the room, trying to summon to mind every police show I had ever seen as I readied myself to explore the unknown. It was unnerving how quiet it was. I crept into the wide hallway, noting that there were about six doorways to my left and a stairway to my right. I inhaled with a soft, shuddering breath before steeling myself enough to continue.

I raised the gun to eye level, feeling pretty damn detective-like, and moved to the first door. I put my ear against it and listened, keeping my eyes on the stairway. Anybody could come down at any second, and I gripped the gun until my knuckles were white. I had never used one seriously before. My father had taken my brothers hunting with him, though, and before they had been allowed to join him, he'd instructed all of us to take a gun safety course to appease my mother. Beyond that I'd never had an interest in them. Now, I was beginning to regret it.

I didn't hear anything inside and pushed the door open. I scanned the room. This was an office of some kind, with a metal desk and an uncomfortable-looking chair. No North. I let the door close as noiselessly as I could before moving on to the next. There were several other empty rooms, and I felt my frustration mounting. I crossed the hall and peeked into the room farthest from the staircase. I let out a soft growl of frustration when the dark room appeared empty as well. Where the hell was she?

Just as I was about to let the door fall closed, I heard a soft gasp of breath. I felt my heart surge with elation and pushed inside without even thinking twice about it. It was so dark that I couldn't even see my own hands in front of me. The windows in here must have been boarded up and well-covered. I heard a slight rustling sound to my left and whipped around, shoving my gun in front of me with a restrained yelp of fear.

"*Finch?*"

"North!"

My voice came out like gravel as the form of the woman I loved came into focus. She was standing in the corner of the room and she rushed to me, throwing her arms over my head. They were still bound, but we embraced tightly as hot tears began to spring into my eyes.

"Thank god." I held her close to my body. "I thought…"

"Aria, you have to get out of here." North's voice was choked but angry. "What the hell were you thinking?"

"I was thinking of you," I said, looking at North with a helpless shrug. "I couldn't just leave you here."

"You could and you will, Aria. It's dangerous. Do you know what they might do to you?"

"I don't care. I have to get you out."

"You don't understand. They can't kill me here. They need me alive. But you? They won't give a shit what happens to you."

I nodded. "Yeah, yeah. I already thought about that."

North smirked at me. "Of course you did. And I imagine you thought you had weighed the risks?"

I nodded again. "I did. I can't leave you, North. I won't go anywhere unless you come with me."

"Damn it, Finch. I wasn't counting on you being this stubborn."

North's tone was sharp, but she was now fully alert, moving briskly through the room. She let the ropes around her wrist drop to the floor, and my eyebrows shot up at her. She lifted the corner of her lip into a smug smile. "I've been working at that for a while."

I pursed my lips, trying not to let my idiotic attraction to her show. There were so many other things to attend to.

"Come on," I said. "I know where there's a window open. We'll get out of here."

North nodded, and I motioned her behind me, holding the gun once again up in front of my face.

"Wait a minute. Where the hell did you get a gun?" North demanded. Her hushed tone did nothing to take the authority out of her voice, and I let myself smile fully this time as I led the way out the door.

"I'll tell you later. Be quiet."

I heard a stifled "*hmph*" from behind me, but, shockingly, she did as I said. We were soon making our way toward the room I had come into.

Clang. Clang. Clang.

North's grip tightened around my arm, and I froze as a long shadow began to descend from the staircase.

"Oh, fuck," I murmured. I looked to North, my eyes wild with fear, and pointed to the doorway of the room I'd broken into. I aimed my gun at the staircase. "Run."

CHAPTER FORTY-SIX

North didn't budge and I turned to face her, my brow drawn in concern. "I'm sorry," I whispered. I planted an urgent, angst-filled kiss on her lips, hoping that it would tell her everything I never got a chance to say, before shoving her toward the doorway.

She let out an anguished cry, and suddenly the noise of the footsteps on the staircase became louder.

"What the hell are you doing out?" a deep man's voice bellowed, echoing down the hallway. It was too late for her to make it to the door. I felt the weight of defeat crash over me and did my best not to hyperventilate. I could feel sweat beginning to bead against my forehead and I swallowed hard. I had to keep it together. It had never been more important. I inhaled and raised the gun back toward the stairs.

"Nothing. I got bored," North retorted. I glared at her and she glared back, motioning for me to duck into one of the rooms to avoid detection. I moved into the doorway, cursing inwardly, hoping I wouldn't have to see anything happen to North. "If you wanted me to stay put, you would have locked the door."

"You know if you leave, we kill the girl. And the other girl! Two girls die for you."

North shot me an agonized look, then kept her eyes directed at the staircase. I managed to conceal myself inside one of the rooms, but kept the door open just enough that I could watch the exchange, keeping my aim on a muscular, stern-faced man who had just come into my view. North backed away from him and gave him a sarcastic, tight-lipped smile.

"Why, Edgar? Why would I leave you *now*? You know how attached I've grown to you all."

"Bite me, Acquati. Get back in your room. We're going to lock it now. I was only gone for a minute, and here you are running around the place like a fuckin' ferret."

North swallowed and I grimaced. She was scared. She was good at acting like she wasn't, but I knew that she was.

When she turned to head toward her room, she looked sidelong at me and gave an almost imperceptible shake of the head. Her eyes warned me not to do anything stupid. I frowned, trying to calculate the risk. Maybe I could wait until this guy was gone and try to get her out again. How many men were there here, anyway? Why was I so terrible at recon?

I heard a sudden shout coming from upstairs, above us, and North froze.

"I said *move*!" he shouted into her face, shoving her down to the ground. North let out a whimper and I realized that she was genuinely injured, whether from the fall or other altercations prior to it, I couldn't say. Either way, she struggled to get back on her feet and the man took the opportunity to slap her on the back of the head and knock her face into the ground.

"Oh, fuck no," I growled, bursting from my hiding place.

"What the hell?" Edgar exclaimed, whipping around to face me. I squeezed my eyes closed at the same time I squeezed the trigger of the gun and felt myself being jerked backward by the recoil as the man let out a loud bellow.

"Rex!"

"Fuck," North groaned. I finally opened my eyes and saw the man slumped down on the ground, holding his shoulder and glaring up at me.

"Rex!" he shouted again.

"You have to get out of here, Aria. They'll kill you," North exclaimed, struggling toward me on the ground. I shook my head, fighting the ringing in my ears so I could understand her."I'm not leaving you."

"Damn it, Finch! This is no time to be stubborn."

Edgar was starting to stagger to his feet, and I heard footsteps rushing down the stairs. North was on her feet first and had her hands around my arm. She tugged me toward the escape route.

"Acquati, what the fuck are you trying to pull?" A new voice caused my blood to turn to ice, and I gaped at the stairwell. A bald man was standing there, glaring down at us with a dark glint in his eyes.

Before I could even comprehend what was happening, he had flown down the rest of the stairwell. I raised the gun and fired, but he had already anticipated my shot and dodged out of the way. I didn't even register his position before I felt a sharp stinging in my hand and the gun flew to the ground. Rex stepped on it and grinned.

"You've got balls for a chick," he said with a snort. "I like that."

I tried to dash away from Rex, my flight instincts finally winning over fight now that I didn't have the gun, but it was too late. I shouted out in pain as Rex moved, fast as lightning, and his hands closed tightly around my neck. I squirmed, struggling to release myself, but I couldn't. The room started to darken as my vision was clouded by a lack of oxygen. I was jerked forward suddenly and saw a glimpse of North's enraged face.

"Get the hell off me!" Rex yelled. I heard a thud as Rex released one hand to land a hard blow. He grinned as North collapsed to the ground and he returned his hand to my neck.

"Finch, no!" North's shout was anguished. I had never heard pain like that in her voice before. I let out a pathetic, gargled sound as I tried to comfort her. I could feel my consciousness slipping and I cursed myself one last time for failing the one person on the planet I cared for the most.

CHAPTER FORTY-SEVEN

"Aria, wake up," North whispered.

I felt cool hands against my face and opened my eyes, my head instantly flooding with pain.

"That didn't go very well," I murmured, doing my best to focus on North. She smiled, a warm expression despite the fact that I could tell that she had been crying. My brow creased and I reached my hand up to her face. "Are you okay?"

She let out a terse laugh. "You're the one who was unconscious, Finch." She paused, her expression haunted, and I wondered if she was reliving the nightmare of what had just happened. In either case, she shook it away and returned her attention to me. "How are you feeling?"

"I'm fine," I said, instinctively bracing my palms on the ground to push myself upright. My strength faltered as I realized I was lying on the cold cement floor. My head was cradled in North's lap, and the rest of me was covered with a tattered piece of cloth that smelled remarkably like her. It must have been what had served as her blanket during her time in captivity. Leave it to North to turn an old rag bougie.

"Stop that," she demanded, easily overtaking my efforts to sit up. "Just rest for a moment."

"Why am I alive?"

"They called Serge, their boss, to see what he wanted to do with you. He said to hold tight until he could come and appraise your value."

"My value…?"

North looked down at me, her expression vacant a moment. "Yes. He also said that if I can't keep you in line until he knows what you're worth, he'll kill you in front of me."

"Oh."

We sat in an awkward silence as my mind tried to reconcile my body's oddly intimate proximity to North's. There was nothing sexual about it. It was strange to feel her comforting me like this after everything that we'd gone through. The confusing weight of the time I had wasted being bound by my mistrust was overwhelming. It had been so long since I thought that I could trust her. I never really knew what to believe. Now, with both of our lives in immediate danger, it was the first time I had really felt safe.

"How did we get here?" I wondered aloud. I had bits and pieces of the terrible whole in mind, but there were still so many unanswered questions. North inhaled deeply, and I felt myself move with her body as she exhaled again.

"We're here, Finch, because you've been helping me to do something that many people are very angry about."

"Slave labor?" I asked, frowning.

North shook her head, repressing a smile. "No, no. Nothing like that." She paused. "Well, actually it *is* related to that…"

I gazed at her expectantly, still feeling too drained to push her for the details.

"A lot of companies, and very rich families, have a lot to lose if their free labor sources were to become limited. St. Peter's is a huge player in all of this, and it was their choice to interfere. They abducted my sister in an effort to get to me. I thought she was dead until I began getting strange photos in the mail."

I frowned, surprised to hear that the company I'd initially interned with would have anything to do with North's situation. "Wait. St. Peter's abducted your sister? Why?"

North sighed. "It turns out their 'green' products are actually very much not. In fact, the materials they use to print their 'love and kindness' T-shirts are bought at an outrageous discount and sewn together with slave labor. They have sweatshops for their cleaning products and detergents. They have sweatshops for their packaging and labels. They have sweatshops for many things. And I'd wager the people they connect to the West via social media are further exploited laborers."

"I always felt like there was something off about them."

"You would have been correct."

I sighed, kicking myself inwardly for having such extreme tunnel vision during the time I'd worked there. The only thought in my head had been building a résumé that would impress a woman like North. No, not a woman like North. Specifically North. I had wanted to impress North. And now we were being held captive in Malaysia by slave laborers due to a corporation that could have been taken down during my internship.

"There is a vigilante organization that was working with one of the countries where this is going on. They realized that things weren't adding up, but St. Peter's had managed to keep their name off everything."

"Vigilantes? You mean the Poison Ivys?"

"Yes," North said. "I assume you're familiar?"

"I did some work for them in college."

North lifted her eyes above my head, her expression that of barely concealed disdain but not of surprise. "Of course you did."

"It's rewarding," I said, frowning defensively.

North allowed a soft hint of a smile. "I'm sure you excelled."

"I did, actually."

"To tell you the truth, it's part of the reason I hired you."

I gazed at North, stupefied, and her hint of a smile blossomed into her true dazzling grin. "I heard about your work with them through my own sources. However, they've really been giving me a hard time." North's smile faltered and I felt another pang of guilt.

"Yeah."

"Aria."

"Hmm?"

"You haven't been working with the Ivys to bring me down for slave labor, have you?"

I blinked. I had been involved with both St. Peter's *and* the Ivys. She had more evidence and reason to be suspicious of me than I had ever had of her. She also had the courage to question my motives outright. My heart palpitated and I tried to read her expression. Did she hate me? No. She was looking at me, gaze level and gentle, arms still protectively surrounding me. I'd just have to be honest.

"No. The Ivys wanted me to help them but I couldn't until I had all the details."

North looked away, failing at her attempt to hide a tender smile. She cleared her throat then returned her gaze to me. "Anyway, St. Peter's determined that it would be safer to knock out two birds with one stone. Shift the blame of their misdeeds, and bring about the downfall of their greatest competitor."

"So they've been setting you up?"

North pursed her lips before continuing. "It was easy to because I have been working with survivors of human trafficking, in many different forms. In fact, Malaysia is the area where I wanted to begin the expansion of my business because it seems the ideal location to help survivors, here at the source. I want to provide refuge for those who have no one else to help them, and doing so locally can help the most people. But it can be very dangerous."

"What did you want to do to help?" I had always heard horror stories about human trafficking, but I'd resigned myself long ago to understanding that it was too elaborate an issue for me to be able to tackle on my own. What good would one person be able to do? North, though, was going out and doing it. She was even more than I had ever thought to believe about her.

"Acquati Technologies can provide jobs—*good* jobs—to these survivors. Malaysia happens to be a hotspot for trafficking. Once I located Levante, I realized that one of the most important things I can do is to intercept those in danger and provide them with refuge, a little like I've attempted to do for her, but on a grander scale. I have been in communication with many social workers and other people who are willing to put everything on the line to help those they suspect are being trafficked. Those people, if all goes well, are offered safe haven, and I am working to set up companies globally that will help them to reinvent themselves and begin again. If that's what they choose."

"Your weird spreadsheets," I mumbled. North smiled down at me.

"My weird spreadsheets. And all of this." Her hand swept out in demonstration at the barren room we were locked inside. "My legacy."

"Are they going to traffic us?"

"Not me," she said softly. "At least not yet. I have no idea what they might want to do with you, though. God, Finch. I really wish you would have just let me go."

"No."

North raised a brow down to me as the quick, labored word left my lips. Letting her go wasn't an option. It never had been.

Even before I had known the truth, I couldn't shake her. Now, I *did* know everything. Finally. I never wanted to let anything get in the way of it again. How could I have been so stupid? Why couldn't I have just trusted her?

I had no choice but to face the entirety of my stupidity with my head in her lap like a helpless, shamed child. It was amazing that she was even speaking to me right now.

"I'm sorry," I said, my voice hushed as I realized with horror that I couldn't stop the tears that were beginning to quake my body. "North…Oh, god."

North allowed me to cry, holding me in a firm embrace that filled me with anguished gratitude. There was so much more softness in her than I had given her credit for. Things hadn't needed to be so complicated. I had, once again, been my own worst enemy.

Finally, I felt North's warm lips, light against my forehead, and she shushed me. "Aria, none of this is your fault. I thought that keeping things to myself would be best, but you should never have been involved at all. I was a fool. And so selfish. I was more focused on achieving my goal than making sure that we would be able to build any real foundation of trust with one another. If our positions were switched, I would have left a long time ago. But you stayed..." North's voice softened. "Aria, you *stayed*. You're amazing."

"Or stupid," I hiccupped.

North let out a small laugh. "You're a brilliant woman, Finch. This is my fault. I thought I was ahead of the curve, that I'd be able to keep you safe. But you're the one who ended up coming to *my* rescue. Of all the idiotic things..."

"See? Stupid!" I insisted.

"No," North murmured, letting her lips brush against my forehead. "No."

The silence that blanketed us now wasn't awkward at all. It was full of a thousand unspoken words, and we allowed them to wash over us, the closeness of our bodies speaking in a language that didn't require translation. The last of my tears dried, and North helped me to sit up and face her.

"Really, Finch. You're incredibly brave. And despite how angry I am that you put yourself at risk, I'm really glad you're with me."

I blinked. There was no way she was calling *me* brave. I had done nothing but run from my feelings for her the entire time I had known her. Just because I was reckless enough to charge in thinking I could save her didn't make me brave. It definitely put me in the category of "stupid," though.

North sighed, leaning her back against the wall behind her. "I can see there's no changing your mind about this, but I think I should remind you that stubbornness and stupidity are often confused for one another."

I couldn't help but crack a smile, and North grinned back, her beautiful face interrupting every thought in my mind with an abrupt appreciation of her.

"So, what do we do now?" I asked, fidgeting beneath her gaze. She offered her hand to me, and when I took it, she squeezed.

"We make it through this. Together."

I nodded, and North held her arm out. I took the cue and snuggled against her, comforted by her nearness. But I wouldn't let it sedate me. We were going to find a way out. There was no other option.

CHAPTER FORTY-EIGHT

I didn't get any sleep, but North was clearly exhausted. Her rest was fitful, however, and at one point she jolted awake and when she saw me, the relief on her face heart-wrenching. She gripped me for a moment before nodding off again. I wondered if she would even remember the moment upon waking. It would haunt me, though.

It was cold; there was no furniture in the room where we were being held captive. We were reduced to huddling against the wall shivering together. The body heat and the makeshift blanket made it bearable, in that sense, anyway. My mind was racing with potential schemes, but nothing seemed realistic. I couldn't just lie down and accept that this could be it for us, but as time wore on, it seemed more and more difficult to believe that we would make it through.

"Rise and shine, pretty ladies."

I froze, my entire body chilled by the abrupt break in the silence. There was a metallic banging on the door where we had been locked up overnight and soon there was a crack of light.

The silhouette of a man entered the room and I winced as my eyes were forced to adjust to the icy glare of a single light bulb on the ceiling. North's body was tense behind me, and she held me closer to her. Neither of us spoke.

"The rumors are true, then. We have your friend now, Acquati."

The man wasn't one I recognized, and there was an emptiness to his expression that gave me goose bumps. He wasn't particularly tall, but with the two of us huddled on the floor together, unarmed and completely at his mercy, he seemed larger than life.

I felt North's tight grip on my biceps, and I didn't feel much comfort from the protective gesture. Especially when the man untucked the glimmering weapon from his pants.

"Tell me, blond girl, who are you?"

"Your worst nightmare."

"Oh my god, Finch."

The man's expression twisted for a moment before he let out a chuckle.

"Plucky, I'll give her that. Maybe I won't kill her right away, though Edgar is begging me to. Did she tell you she shot Edgar? He'll be fine, she's a terrible shot, but still. Very rude."

"I was there, Serge."

I felt the sudden pressure of cold metal against my neck. He was caressing my face with the muzzle of his gun. "You should have stopped her," he said severely. "Finch, is it?"

I offered a reluctant nod, too stubborn to break my composure. What did I have to lose? At least if he killed me, North wouldn't remember my grand finale as a sniveling ball of fear on the floor.

"Hmm. Would you like to come home with me, Finch?"

"Fuck off, Serge!" North shouted.

Serge chuckled heartily before returning his attention back to me. "Oh, the big boss woman likes you. That makes this so much better."

I glanced nervously over my shoulder to North, whose jaw was set. Her fingers were still tight around me. If he tried to make a move against me, I knew that she was going to get herself killed trying to stop it. I had to de-escalate the situation somehow.

"If you're happy and you know it, clap your hands..."

Why the hell I decided bursting into song would be the solution to our life-threatening situation, I'll never know, but sing I did. With gusto.

"Is she always like this?" Serge asked, raising a brow at North.

I continued singing and heard the exasperation in North's exhale. It probably would have made me laugh under other circumstances.

"She's more of a cuckoo bird than a finch," Serge said. "I'm here to give you a choice, cuckoo bird."

My singing faltered, and once again North's fingers were tight around my arm.

Serge took a step closer and leaned down to grin into my face. I could feel his breath as he spoke and did my best not to recoil. "Do you want to be a working girl or a *working* girl? My evaluation is concluded. You have a screw loose, but you're too pretty to waste."

I blinked as the implications of his question struck me.

"I already have a job."

Serge's face contorted before breaking into a sinister smile and he gave a nod. "I see," he said, standing upright and turning toward the door. "The choice is up to me."

Neither North nor I dared to move until the door slammed behind him, leaving us in suffocating darkness.

CHAPTER FORTY-NINE

"North…"

It had been about an hour since Serge's visit, and my eyes had managed to adjust to the pitch-black room once again. I struggled to my feet, holding a hand to my temple as I was overcome by brief dizziness. "North…"

North stood with me, taking hold of me to keep me steady, then placed a single finger over her lips. "Come on," she whispered. "I'm getting you out of here before this gets too out of hand."

I opened my mouth to reply, but she shook her head and I clamped it shut again. I followed her as we crept to the door. I was surprised when it opened easily in her hands.

"How?" I mouthed. North pointed to the latch of the door and I saw that she had managed to pull enough tape from the bindings on her wrist to compress it and keep it from locking. I shook my head, impressed, before she motioned me forward. I followed, though there was a part of me that was reluctant. I didn't like the way she'd said she was going to get *me* out of

there. She should have been saying that *we* were going to get out of there. Then again, if I didn't think that she had any intention of escaping herself, then she wouldn't have been learning to navigate her prison like a mini MacGyver.

I wasn't going to give her the option of staying. We would get out of there together, just as she'd said.

I expected the corridor to be guarded, but once again, they seemed to have forgotten about us. However, I could hear voices in the distance and the thud of footsteps over our heads. North paused to listen and then continued. I followed, unsure of what to expect. My heart seized in fear when my foot brushed against a piece of debris on the floor and a small clattering noise echoed throughout the room. I was positive that they would hear that and come rushing down again. They had already shown no hesitation in harming both of us, and the grim possibilities loomed over me.

Nothing happened, however. North continued on, and I realized for the first time that she wasn't wearing shoes. It was bizarre for the familiar clicking of her heels to be absent. It was for the best, though. My own weathered, cloth sneakers didn't make very much noise, unless the floor was wet or sticky. Then they gave an impressive squeak.

"You two don't learn."

Serge's icy voice froze us in our tracks. I didn't even have the chance to turn around before his hands were wrapped around my neck. My eyes watered as I tried to fight him off.

"Why is everyone choking me?"

"It's cleaner," Serge said with a sickening smile.

"*Stop it!* Aria!"

North dove at us to try to get me out of his grasp, but he kicked her away with no effort at all. She flew backward and crashed into a pile of metal barrels. It was deafening as they clattered to the ground. My voice came out in a gargle as I tried to call her name, but it was easily lost in the noise. Not that it would have helped her any...

"You are more trouble than you're worth, cuckoo bird. We will get rid of you to teach the boss lady a lesson, as promised, then lock her in a real fucking cage."

North groaned in pain. I tried to reach for her, but I was losing air fast. My body was growing heavy, and the vision of North faded as white bubbles overcame my vision.

Just as I thought that it was all over for me, I heard a familiar voice at the top of the staircase. I was too delirious to comprehend what it was saying, but suddenly my face was splattered with blood and the death grip on my neck had been released. Serge slumped to the ground, and I wavered on my feet. Before I fell, Thom was clutching me in his arms.

He curled me close to his body and rushed over to North, helping her to her feet. He kept his arm around me and hit a button on a walkie-talkie he'd released from the vest he was wearing.

"All clear. We need a medic. One dead and two injured."

"Copy," a static-filled voice chirped before promptly dissipating.

"Shit, Aria," Thom said, his eyes wide as he peered down into my face. "What the hell are you doing here?"

"Is she okay?" North asked, scrambling desperately toward me.

"I—" Before I could say anything to reassure her, North had buried her face into my neck and unleashed a heart-wrenching sob. My entire body was weak and heavy, but I draped my arms around her and held her tightly.

"I'm so sorry, Aria. I should never have gotten you involved. I had no idea you would…"

She broke off and continued crying against me. I held her close as Thom served as an awkward stabilizing force that kept the two of us propped on our feet while we embraced.

"Stop apologizing," I whispered, my voice hoarse. "I would do anything for you."

Her tears didn't stop coming, and soon we were surrounded by paramedics who were speaking rapidly in Malay to Thom. I still hadn't fully comprehended what had happened until they separated me from North. All I had been able to see was her, and when I was left sitting in the back of an ambulance alone with Thom, things really started sinking in.

"Aria, do you know how stupid that was?" he exclaimed once we were alone. "I had to have my men move in early. We weren't ready yet—I'm not even sure that we'll have enough evidence to convict!"

"What are you talking about?" I croaked.

I stared at Sketchy Thom, the IT guy with pictures of my wounded lover in his dirty little apartment. His men? I looked around, slowly realizing that he wasn't just my sort-of boyfriend thing or someone trying to kill North. He was kind of a cop.

Thom looked at me like I was an idiot, and then let out a low sigh. "Look. I don't know how to tell you this..." He sighed. "I've been working undercover, investigating St. Peter's."

"St. Peter's? Not North?"

"Well, I had to make sure she was innocent first. I investigated the obvious leads, but we realized that they wanted to frame your boss for some pretty underhanded shit."

"That would have been nice to know a month ago."

Thom shifted. "I'm sure. It's confidential though, you know? I had to get close to you to figure out whether or not Acquati was guilty. I followed the trail here and realized that she and her sister are the victims here. We've been setting up to save them and take down the whole ring."

"Wait..." I blinked slowly. "So, you were only dating me to investigate North?"

Thom's face reddened, and he looked down at his hands. "Aria, I really didn't mean for you to get attached to me. I thought for sure you didn't care, and it just seemed like the easiest way to get the information I needed. Then things started getting really dangerous, and I thought I'd be able to protect you if you were nearby."

I blinked at Thom as I attempted to process the information he was giving me. Even though I was fully devoted to North, it felt like a punch in the gut. Before, I'd been considering him as a potential partner, someone I could build a future with, and he'd been using me the whole time? Even before I had slept with North? I didn't want it to hurt, but it did. I'd trusted him, but he might easily have dumped me once he'd gotten the information he needed. And he'd slept with me. What if I hadn't ended up with the most incredible outcome and had been hoping for something more? Maybe my preoccupation with North made us even. At least I didn't have to feel guilty anymore. Or suspicious of anyone. I couldn't figure out a reply, so he kept talking.

"I'm so glad that you agreed to come to Malaysia, which actually turned out to be the *most* dangerous thing in the world for you. I didn't expect you to just go all balls-to-the-wall-rescue-mission. Badass, by the way."

"Thanks."

"Honestly, though, you'd been so distant that it was kind of surprising. Especially since…" He glanced to North, blushing to his ears. "I mean…I do like you, but I understood pretty early on that she's a…priority of yours."

Now it was my turn to blush, caught off guard by memories of all the times I'd ignored Thom or stood him up or straight-up left our date for North. "If I mean more to you than I thought, then I just…well, either way, I'm so sorry I wasn't honest with you."

He ventured to look up at me, his face twisted with anguish. I blinked hard again before a bubble of laughter erupted from deep in my belly. Thom's eyes widened and he looked around frantically. "Where's the medic?" He raised his voice. "I think she's hysterical, can we get some help?"

Before I knew what was happening, North had fought her way away from her own team of paramedics and police officers and was panting in front of me. When she saw my face, she narrowed her eyes.

"Finch."

I swallowed a final peal of laughter and looked at North sheepishly.

"What in the hell has gotten into you?" she asked, placing a hand on her hip. She was looking better now; there was color in her face, and she could stand without swaying. My lips twitched into another smile.

"North, I'd like you to meet Thom."

She furrowed her brow in confusion for a moment, then glanced to my supposed boyfriend. Finally, realization dawned on her. "Thom…Wait, you two know each other?"

Thom offered North a sheepish smile. "Guilty."

In a move that shocked us all, North took the tissue she was gripping and slapped him across the face with it. "What kind of man doesn't feed a helpless little cat?"

I snorted and looked down at my hands. Thom stared at North for a moment, then looked over at me, eyes wide. I glanced back to North, who had already climbed into the ambulance to sit beside me. She took my hand in hers and settled a steel gaze upon the black-hearted man.

It was Thom's turn to blink. He was quiet for a moment. I had a sudden realization of what he must be thinking. I'd already whisked Bilbo away to my own hotel room, but Thom probably hadn't even noticed that my fluffy little buddy was gone. I had a sudden sadistic urge to mess with him. Call it revenge for his neglect and the whole, 'I was only dating you to get info on your boss' thing.

"Thom, please tell me you fed Bilbo today."

Thom froze, put on the spot before his excuse burst forth. "I was being held captive by human traffickers!"

I blinked at him. "You were being held captive by human traffickers?"

"You were being held captive by human traffickers?"

"See, Finch? Black heart."

"North. He saved our lives."

"Well, yeah, but…" North looked lost a moment, and I realized that this was the first—and possibly last—time I'd seen her feeling insecure.

"Don't worry, North. He was just using me to investigate you." I let out another giggle. "We will not be eloping."

North shook her head and sighed. "Well."

I nodded. "Well."

Thom blew out a deep breath. "Well…"

We were allowed a moment of silence before a group of police officers crowded around us.

"We need to ask you a few questions, if you're up to it," a large man with a sweaty brow said in perfect English. "Both of you."

North squeezed my hand and climbed out of the ambulance. She glanced over her shoulder, fixing a killer smile on me. "You heard the man, Finch. Let's get this over with."

EPILOGUE

"Aren't you sick of seeing yourself on TV, Finch?"

North walked briskly past me, gifting me a wry smile on her way to her new favorite perch: the massive windows of our A-frame cabin.

"I'm looking at *you*," I replied. The news stations were still buzzing about St. Peter's being shut down and the ongoing lawsuit that had resulted from it. After recovering North and me and the box she'd left me, they had gotten more than enough evidence for a conviction. We were nearing the end of the storm at last, and North somehow stood to become even more wealthy than before. She had insisted on offering me representation as well, so it seemed my trauma might come with a price tag of its own.

"Did they capture my good side?"

"Which one?" I asked, ignoring North's snort to glance at my watch. "Are you sure it's not too late to cancel?"

"Finch, we're not canceling on your mother. All Nonna has been talking about is our families meeting. It would break her heart."

Now that everything had come to light, North's family had reunited. Levante was still Levante, of course, but she no longer felt like an outcast, which was a start to mending their strained family ties.

"Great, bring the sweet old lady into it. You're hitting below the belt with this whole guilt-trip thing."

"Stop pouting. We made a commitment."

I clicked the television set off and sighed. "But I don't wanna..."

Even Bilbo protested, jumping from my lap to waddle to his food dish, which remained ever-plentiful now that I had been replaced by my lover as his favorite.

North's soft chuckle reached me from across the room. "Come here, you big baby."

She patted the window seat where she had taken up residence, and I got up from the couch to trudge toward her. North opened her arms invitingly to me, and I took my place against her body.

"Everything is going to be fine. Your mother has made a lot of progress."

"That's only because you're a bajillionaire."

North laughed. "Stop that. We're both doing pretty well for ourselves. She's proud of you."

That much was true, at least. Since the whole fiasco in Malaysia, North had decided to move her central headquarters to New York City to be closer to Nonna. We were a little bit over city life, though, so we ended up moving about an hour away to a more rural area, and the nature had been cathartic for the both of us. It was strange to see North living a (somewhat) modest lifestyle, but she had immediately seemed happier. The area suited us both, and since then, I'd been working with North's company, but through my own start-up.

Working for her had been great, but now that we were also living together I didn't want any cries of nepotism to sour the workplace, and I wanted to prove my worth on my own. I had finally begun to realize my passion and pursued it to the fullest.

To my surprise, it was going really well, and not just because North had been the first person to enlist in my services.

The Poison Ivys had contacted me with their apologies and a few job requests of their own, and I'd taken them on gladly. I hadn't realized how much I'd missed the thrill of using my skillset on a whole other level. Data entry and IT was great, but could they compare to digital sleuthing? Not even close. I was back in my element after finding North, and I realized that while I admired North and her work ethic, I could apply my own work ethic to my own work *and* still admire her. All night and several times, if I wanted to. She could still inspire me, but I didn't want to be her. I just wanted to be better.

I rolled my eyes, resigning myself to my bleak future with the families, and North wrapped her arms around me in a snug embrace.

"I love you. You know that, right? I have for so long."

North's soft brown eyes caught mine, and I smiled at her. It wasn't the first time she'd told me, but she wasn't often outwardly sentimental.

"I really love you too."

"Good."

North's scent surrounded me as she leaned down to kiss first my cheek, then my forehead. My eyes fluttered closed as I felt her lips against my temple. They lingered there for a moment before she pulled away.

"You don't have to stop," I murmured, lost in the happy daze of her nearness.

"Oh, really?"

"We still have a few hours before anyone gets here."

North, the master of all things date and time, raised her brow at me. "I hadn't noticed." She tilted my face gently toward hers. Her soft lips took mine in a long, slow kiss that left me sizzling. She pulled away for a moment. "Well, I won't stop if you won't."

"Pff…" I couldn't manage anything more verbal than that.

North grinned against my lips as my body awakened against her touch. I climbed into her lap, caressing her as we kissed.

North inhaled sharply and pulled away to look at me, her eyes smoldering, but serious. “Are you sure, Finch? The neighbors will see.”

I took North’s hands and placed them on my thighs as I sank down against her. North moaned, and I let my lips linger against her ear. “I can assure you, they won’t.”

Bella Books, Inc.

Women. Books. Even Better Together.

P.O. Box 10543
Tallahassee, FL 32302

Phone: 800-729-4992
www.bellabooks.com